STEPSISTERS AT WAR

"A back somi dismount?" Maya walked into the kitchen wearing a warm-up suit over a black leotard. "I am going to use one too."

"What?" Kelly stared at Maya. "I told you at lunch the other day that I was going to try the back somi. Why didn't you say anything?"

Maya shook her head and shrugged. "It didn't seem important," she said. "I often used that dismount in Russia."

"You did?" It sounded as if she had mastered it, while Kelly was still working on it.

"Sure." Maya seemed unconcerned. "Why are you upset? In Russia we often did the same things as each other."

"You're not in Russia anymore, Maya," Kelly snapped. "In case you haven't noticed." Throwing down her dishtowel, she flung open the basement door and stomped downstairs to their home gym.

AMERICAN GOLD GYMNASTS

by Gabrielle Charbonnet

Competition Fever

BANTAM BOOKS
NEW YORK • TORONTO • LONDON • SYDNEY • AUCKLAND

RL 5, 008–012
COMPETITION FEVER
A *Skylark Book* / *June 1996*

ISBN 0-553-48295-5

Published simultaneously in the United States and Canada

Bantam Books are published by Bantam Books, a division of
Bantam Doubleday Dell Publishing Group, Inc. Its trademark,
consisting of the words "Bantam Books" and the portrayal of a
rooster, is Registered in U.S. Patent and Trademark Office and in
other countries. Marca Registrada. Bantam Books, 1540 Broadway,
New York, New York 10036.

PRINTED IN THE UNITED STATES OF AMERICA

OPM   0 9 8 7 6 5 4 3 2 1

With love to my family

Chapter One

"Oh, very nice, Ms. Hales," Kelly Reynolds said as she made a viewfinder out of one hand and pretended to film her pretty African American friend. "Very daring, the way you climbed up on that beam. Now let's see something *really* risky."

Monica Hales gave a big toothy smile. With exaggerated movements, she stood up on the regulation-height balance beam. "For my first trick," she said breathlessly, "I will attempt the dramatic Hales Maneuver. Please watch carefully." With huge flourishes, Monica leaned down, bent her knees, and tucked her head on the side of the beam. Then she rolled forward and ended up in a sitting position. She threw both hands in the air in a touchdown gesture. "Ta-daa!"

Laughing, Kelly clapped hard, then pretended to film some more. "There you have it, folks: the death-defying Hales Maneuver. Otherwise known as a forward somersault. Kids, don't try this at home."

1

"Yeah," Monica laughed. "We're trained professionals."

It was a Tuesday afternoon at Sugarloaf Gymnastic Academy, affectionately called SGA, the training gym that Kelly's mother, Emma Stanton, owned in the Sugarloaf suburb of Atlanta. The two girls had come to class early to get in some extra practice.

Monica slid down to the floor mat and brushed her hands off. "Your turn. I'll film you." She batted her eyes. "It'll be such a treat to film the number-one Silver Star at SGA. A real honor."

"I don't know that you can film anything," Kelly said. "I think your leotard may have broken the camera. Where in the world did you find a purple leopard print leotard?"

"Schiffer's," Monica said, referring to a sporting-goods store at the Sugarloaf Mall. "Where else?" She looked through the imaginary camera as Kelly climbed up on the beam. "Here she is, ladies and gremlins, Kelllllly Reynolds!"

Kelly went into a simple straddle split, gripping each side of the four-inch-wide beam. Because no adult was spotting them, she wasn't allowed to do anything but simple moves.

"So, Ms. Reynolds," Monica said, "how does it feel to be a gold-medal Olympic champion? I understand you were considered the best gymnast in your class when you were little."

"Oh, yes," Kelly said in a perky voice, trying to look as if she'd just won a gold medal. "Gymnastics is my life. Much more important than breathing. And now I'd like to thank

2

my coach and my mom. Who are one and the same person."

"And your coach and your stepfather," Monica added. "Who are one and the same person too."

Kelly looked down at Monica, her eyes meeting Monica's. "Weird, isn't it?" she said in her regular voice.

"I'll say," Monica agreed. "How does it feel so far? It's been two whole weeks since your mom got married."

Remaining in a straddle split, Kelly absently nibbled on her thumbnail. Across the gym, a class of younger students ended their lesson and started to file toward the locker rooms.

"Well, it's . . . weird," Kelly said finally. She swung her legs around to perch on the side of the beam facing Monica. "It's been just the two of us for so long," she said, giving a little laugh. "For ten years, it's been me and Mom, and Mom and me. Now all of a sudden, it's me and Mom and Dimitri and Maya."

Kelly's parents had divorced when she was two years old, and her mother, Emma Stanton, had taken back her maiden name. Kelly didn't remember her father. She knew he was a businessman who didn't understand Emma's devotion to gymnastics. He sent Kelly Christmas and birthday cards, but otherwise he was a complete stranger to her.

Monica nodded understandingly. "I know," she said. "Even though Emma and Dimitri have been dating for a long time, it doesn't seem real. 'Cause he was in Russia and she was here. And then, boom! They get married, and now you're in a ready-made family."

3

"Yeah." Kelly jumped off the beam and went over to the big floor mat area. She did a couple of cartwheels and roundoffs to loosen up. "I guess I'm getting used to it," she said, coming back to stand by Monica. "I really like Dimitri —he's sweet. And he's great to Mom. But I'm not used to having a dad. Or a sister. And now I have both."

Dimitri Resnikov was a world-famous gymnastics coach who had trained four Olympic medalists. Kelly thought it was really romantic the way her mother and Dimitri had met when Emma was only fourteen and Dimitri was eighteen. They had both been competing in the 1972 Olympics —Emma for the United States and Dimitri for what was then the Soviet Union. Emma had won a silver medal in the vault, and Dimitri had come in fourth on the still rings —just a few hundredths of a point shy of getting a medal. Then they hadn't seen each other for twenty years. During that time, Emma and Kelly's father had married, then divorced, and Dimitri's wife had died of a blood disease. When Emma and Dimitri had met again several years ago, they were both coaching gymnasts who were competing in the World Championships. This time they fell in love. And just two weeks ago they had gotten married. Before the wedding, Kelly had never met Dimitri's daughter, Maya.

"That must be really strange," Monica said. "I've always wanted a sister. All I have is boring old Gene." Monica's older brother, Gene, was a sophomore in high school. Kelly and Monica thought he was a total computer nerd. "But now you've got Maya, who's our age. And she's into gymnastics. It's like a dream come true."

"I thought it would be cool too," Kelly said. "You know, a sister to do stuff with, talk to, go shopping with . . ." Her forehead creased, and a troubled look came over her face. Glancing around to make sure no one could hear her, she moved closer to Monica. "But it isn't really turning out the way I had thought," she whispered. "I mean, I guess Maya's nice and all. But we're totally different. It's like she's from another planet or something."

Monica grinned. "Well, she *is* from Russia. Can't get more different than that."

Sighing, Kelly tapped one bare foot against the floor mat. "I guess. But I keep trying to be her friend, and she doesn't seem interested. I asked her to go to the mall, and she said she didn't need anything." Kelly made a face. "As if *that* has anything to do with going to the mall! Then last night I was trying to explain the different plots of *Kiss Yesterday Good-bye,* and she just sat there with a blank look on her face."

Monica frowned. She and Kelly loved to watch *Kiss Yesterday Good-bye.* It was their favorite TV show. "Did you tell her about how Ryan had kidnapped Marcy? And how Stephanie was blackmailing Frederick and Junior?"

"Uh-huh." Kelly nodded. "She didn't seem to get it."

"Geez." Monica pinched her lip between her forefinger and thumb, the way she usually did when she was thinking. "Well, hang in there," she advised. "Y'all have to live together."

"I know," Kelly said. "Maybe we need more time to get used to each other."

5

"Sure," Monica said. "Two weeks is nothing."

"You're right. I bet Maya will be really nice when I get to know her. Dimitri sure is," Kelly said with a smile. "And he's a fabulous coach too. We're lucky to have him here." Then her smile faded. "All the same, it's hard having to share Mom with other people. No matter how nice they are."

Chapter  Two

"Listen up, people," Emma Stanton called from one end of the gym. "Gold Stars over here by the floor mats. Silver Stars warm up by the barre." She glanced around and saw Kelly and Monica. "Where are the other Silver Stars? I saw only Maya in the locker room." Absently she patted her wavy brown hair into place. Today she was wearing a navy blue warm-up jacket with the SGA logo embroidered on it in gold thread.

"They'll be here," Kelly answered. "They still have two minutes till class."

Emma looked at her watch, then smiled at Kelly. "You're right. It's nice that you girls came early to get ready."

Smiling proudly, Kelly and Monica headed over to the ballet barre along the mirrored wall.

A minute later Maya joined them and immediately began stretching. She was wearing a long-sleeved black leotard, and her blond hair was tightly braided and looped up to be out of her way.

"Hey, Maya," Kelly said. "I didn't see you after school. I waited for you."

Maya didn't break her rhythm. "My history teacher kept us late," she said in her lightly accented English. Her blue eyes never left the mirror as she stretched first one leg and then the other.

"How's school going, Maya?" Monica asked. "You know, since we're in the same science class, if you ever want to get together and study, I'd be glad to help you."

"Science is easy for me," Maya said abruptly. She bent low from the waist and placed her palms flat on the floor.

"O-kaay," Monica said slowly. She met Kelly's eyes in the mirror and raised her eyebrows. Kelly shrugged.

Moving through her basic warm-up routine, Kelly watched the rest of the gym reflected in the mirror. Her own image showed a small, wiry twelve-year-old, with dark brown hair pulled back in a ponytail. Behind her, several classes were going on at once. The Gold Stars were on the floor mats, and the Bronze Stars were finishing a tumbling exercise.

At SGA, students were divided into teams. The youngest team, the Twinklers, consisted of four- and five-year-olds. Kelly had been a Twinkler before she was even in kindergarten. Then there were the Copper Stars, who were six to eight years old. Bronze Stars were between eight and ten, and the Silver Stars were eleven, twelve, and thirteen years old.

Gymnasts fourteen years old and up were Gold Stars. Everyone in this elite group was usually aiming to compete in the Olympics. Kelly couldn't wait to be a Gold Star. She could already see herself competing in the National and World Championships, and then in the pre-Olympic trials. . . .

Maya finished her work at the bar and started doing practice handstands on the mats nearby.

"That girl needs to lighten up," Monica said softly.

"She's very serious about gymnastics," Kelly said, feeling a need to defend her new stepsister.

"So are you—you were the state champion for your age last year. But at least you're polite to people," Monica grumbled.

Kelly shrugged again. She didn't know what to say. Maybe Maya was having trouble adjusting to all the changes too. Shaking her head, Kelly concentrated on getting all her muscles warm and loose.

A deep sigh of satisfaction escaped her as she started doing deep knee bends. Class was about to start, and she was in her favorite place in the whole world. Every time she walked through the double glass doors, she got excited about gymnastics all over again. She loved the smells of rosin, leather, plastic, chalk, and even sweat—it all made her heart beat a little faster.

Emma had bought the building, a warehouse outside

Atlanta, right after her divorce. Inside, the gym was one huge open room, full of gymnastics equipment—uneven parallel bars, balance beams, vaults, pommel horses, still rings hanging from the ceiling, a trampoline, and mats.

In the front of the building were Emma's office, the first-aid room, a waiting area, and Dimitri's office. In the back were the locker rooms, bathrooms, a locked room for more equipment, and the hangout room. The hangout room had tables and comfortable chairs, in case anyone needed to do homework before or after class. There were also a couple of vending machines: one for juice and one for healthful snacks, like dried fruit, plain crackers, pretzels, and unsalted nuts. Emma also kept a big bowl of fresh fruit on one of the tables.

All along one wall of the gym were enormous floor-to-ceiling windows. The opposite wall, where Kelly, Maya, and Monica were warming up, was lined with mirrors, and a ballet barre ran its entire length. Most of the gymnasts also took dance classes to help develop grace and coordination.

Now Kelly put one leg up on the barre and leaned over slowly, feeling the pull in the backs of her knees. Next to her, Monica swept downward in a big stretch that let her puffy, dark brown ponytail trail along the floor.

"Whoa, am I late?" Candace Stiles blew in through the front doors like a whirlwind, followed by her twin sister, Kathryn. They were Silver Stars too.

Kelly checked the clock on the far wall. "Amazingly

enough, you have fifteen seconds to spare," she told Candace.

Candace had bright red hair and green eyes. Sometimes Kelly felt as if Candace were a bee, buzzing around all the time. She was really nice, but she got bored easily, talked a lot, made jokes, and was often late to class. Dimitri had started calling her the Red Whirlwind.

Even though they were twins, Kathryn was incredibly different. She had dark red hair and hazel eyes, and she was very serious. They were both in sixth grade at Sugarloaf Middle School, a year below Kelly, Monica, and now Maya. Kathryn had been taking gymnastics almost as long as Kelly had, which was practically forever. Sometimes they had been in the same Star group, sometimes not. This year Kathryn had become a Silver Star, when she turned eleven. She was focused and determined and worked hard at her routines and skills.

Candace, on the other hand, had started taking gymnastics only five months before. Kathryn still called it her twin's hobby of the week. At first Candace had been a Bronze Star, but she learned quickly, and just three weeks earlier Emma had made her a Silver Star.

"Hello, hello. Have to change." Hiroko Kobayashi rushed past them, her chin-length black hair swinging against her cheeks. "Back in a sec," she called over her shoulder.

"Gosh, something must have happened," Monica said, standing up and switching legs.

"I know what you mean," Kelly said. "I don't think Harry's ever been late before in her life."

Maya looked over. "It's bad to be late," she said in her clipped accent.

"I'm sure Harry has a good reason," Kelly said in surprise. She sat down on a floor mat and spread her feet wide, pointing her toes. Then she leaned over and slowly tried to touch her forehead to the ground.

Hiroko—known as Harry—was the last member of the Silver Stars. Like Candace and Kathryn, she was eleven and in sixth grade at Sugarloaf Middle School. She was Japanese American. Her gymnastics had really improved over the last year.

In just two minutes Harry was back in a pale pink leotard. Her hair was pulled off her face with a matching pale pink headband. Instantly she dropped to the ground next to Kelly and started stretching.

"What happened?" Kelly asked, standing up and stretching her arms overhead as high as they'd go. "Is everything okay?"

Harry rolled her eyes. "Yeah. I had to stay late to talk to my teacher about my math test. It's no big deal. I just have to schedule a makeup. But he kept me waiting."

A minute later Emma came up and clapped her hands. "Okay, Silver Stars. Are you warmed up?"

"Yes, Emma," Kelly and the others chorused.

"Good," Emma said. "Then let's begin class."

Chapter Three

"I want to see some perfect cartwheels," Emma said, pointing to the long row of mats that went almost the whole way across the gym.

The Silver Stars formed one straight line, and Candace started off. Kelly knew that anyone watching would think cartwheels sounded really boring—after all, they were gymnasts! They could do all kinds of harder things, but Kelly had learned that you had to do even small, unimportant things with concentration and perfect form. In competition, someone could do a whole line of perfect aerial cartwheels—with no hands—but if her front somersault was sloppy, the judges took points off.

"Good," Emma said when Maya had finished her line. "Now some front walkovers."

Maya walked to the first mat and concentrated for a moment. Then she put both hands down, one right after the other, and followed smoothly with her body and legs.

13

Her feet landed softly on the mat, one right after the other, like her hands.

"Excellent, Maya," Emma said. "You made a nice, even circle. Very good. Do some forward and some backward, okay?"

Maya didn't smile but nodded curtly. Down the mats she went, doing one perfect walkover after another.

Monica's right, Kelly thought. *Maya has to lighten up. This isn't boot camp. She doesn't have to do things like a machine.*

Kelly waited for her turn to do walkovers. They were one of the first things she had learned how to do. She couldn't imagine *not* knowing how to do them. But she knew the Twinklers and some of the Copper Stars were struggling to learn them.

Harry started down the line of mats, and Kelly got into position. They began each class this way: with simple exercises designed to warm them up, stretch their muscles, and get their minds focused. Emma always said that a person's mental attitude was just as important as her physical skill. Sometimes even more important.

Silver Star classes met from three-thirty to five-thirty on Tuesdays, Wednesdays, and Thursdays, and from ten to noon on Saturdays. Mondays and Fridays they had off, but Kelly often came to SGA anyway, just to stretch and hang out, and to watch the Gold Stars. The Gold Stars had to come six days a week, for two hours each weekday and four hours on Saturday. The gym was closed on Sundays.

Emma clapped her hands again. "Okay, guys, good.

14

Candace, I'm seeing real improvement, but try to be exact and precise with every single movement. And remember one word—"

Kelly and the rest of the Silvers knew what was coming. "Form!" they shouted.

Emma grinned. "That's right. Form counts for a lot. Harry, you had excellent form today. And Maya, you had perfect extension on those roundoffs."

Harry beamed. Maya nodded.

Kelly waited for her mother to say something nice to her. She had been trying hard to have perfect form too. But Emma didn't say a word. She didn't always compliment people. But if someone messed up, they got corrected one hundred percent of the time. Kelly was glad that at least Emma hadn't corrected her.

"Hi, Dimitri," Kelly called as her new stepfather came over to them.

"Hi, Dimitri," the rest of the Silver Stars chimed. All except Maya. Kelly noticed that Maya only gave her father a tiny smile.

"Hi, girls," Dimitri said. His Russian accent was much stronger than Maya's.

The Silver Stars grinned as Dimitri put one arm around Emma's waist. She smiled at him, and Kelly snickered.

"What are the Silver Stars doing today?" Dimitri asked in his rumbly voice.

Emma consulted her clipboard. "They're going to work with Susan on the trampoline."

"Ugh," Monica said under her breath. "General Lu."

Kelly grinned. She knew Monica was just kidding. Susan Lu was Emma's assistant. She had been a top-rated gymnast until a few years before, when she had broken her ankle during a World Championship performance. Now she taught alongside Emma and Dimitri. Kelly liked her and thought she was a good teacher, but she was very strict. And because she had hurt herself so badly, she was a real stickler for safety, safety, safety at all times.

"Good," Dimitri said. "Then you are with the Gold Stars, and I am with the boys. Right?"

"That's right," Emma said, smiling into his eyes.

"Emma and Dimitri," Monica sang under her breath, "sitting in a tree, K-I-S-S—"

"Oh, come on," Kelly whispered. "They've only been married two weeks." She tried to catch Maya's eye to grin at her, but Maya was looking straight ahead, like a tin soldier.

Oh, well. Kelly headed across the gym and climbed up on the big trampoline in the middle of the floor.

"Hold on, Kelly," her mother called. "Wait until Susan gets there." She and Dimitri headed off together, talking in low voices, their heads bent close to each other.

"It's so romantic," Candace gushed. "I mean, true love has conquered everything—two different countries, two different worlds. It's practically like *Romeo and Juliet*. Don't you think so, Maya?"

Maya frowned slightly. "They're our teachers," she said. "It's not good to talk about them that way." Folding her arms, she stood stiffly at the side of the trampoline.

16

"They're also your parents," Monica said. "And they just got married. It *is* romantic."

Maya didn't meet Monica's eye. Kelly thought Maya looked uncomfortable.

"It's disrespectful to make personal comments about them, that's all," Maya said.

Monica looked up at Kelly. Kelly made an "oh, boy" kind of face. She just couldn't figure Maya out.

Chapter Four

"Here I am," Susan Lu called, walking swiftly toward the Silver Stars. She still had the tiniest trace of a limp because of her injury. Today her shiny dark hair was pulled into a bouncy ponytail, and she was wearing a trim white warm-up suit and white sneakers.

"Okay, let's see," she said, consulting her own clipboard. "Today let's work on your straddle jumps."

"I love the trampoline," Candace said, tucking a stray strand of hair back into its bun. She was wearing a bright crimson leotard that clashed with her red curls. "Too bad it isn't a competitive event."

Kathryn rolled her eyes. "It's just for training," she reminded her sister. "Working on the tramp helps you practice dismounts and flips and stuff you need in other events."

Candace looked hurt. "I know that. I *am* a Silver Star, you know. It's not like I'm a Twinkler."

General Lu—Susan—spoke over them. "Kelly, begin, please. And let's see some clean lines. Remember, your body is your means of artistic expression. Use it."

Kelly began bouncing, gently at first, then higher and higher. To do a straddle jump, she bounced way up in the air, then split her legs out to the sides and touched her toes. She loved bouncing high; the feeling of freedom and weightlessness was fabulous. Her ponytail was flopping up and down and she felt light and happy. She did three straddle jumps, stretching her legs out as wide as she could, keeping her toes pointed and her knees straight.

"Hey, Monica," she said, panting, between bounces. "Remember when you wanted to be an astronaut?"

Monica laughed, looking up at her. "You think you can touch the moon from there?" she teased.

When Kelly was at her highest, she could see the whole gym. The Gold Stars were working with Emma on their floor routine. Some of them were watching Kelly. Dimitri was on the other side of the gym with some of the boys. Kelly grinned. Wait until Monica was up here. She'd be able to see Beau Jarrett on the parallel bars. Monica had a total crush on Beau Jarrett.

After a couple more straddle jumps, Susan motioned Kelly down.

Next Susan gave Maya a leg up, and Maya walked to the middle of the tramp. Her face expressionless, she began to bounce higher and higher.

"I can't believe someone can jump on the tramp and still

look like they're not having fun," Kelly whispered to Monica.

Monica giggled.

Then Maya began a series of perfect extended straddle jumps. She got great height, her splits were perfect, her toes pointed. *Talk about clean lines,* Kelly thought. Everything Maya did was perfectly crisp and clean and precise. An uncomfortable feeling came over Kelly. She had been taking gymnastics practically since she could walk. And her Olympic medal-winning mother was a great coach. So Kelly was used to being incredibly good at gymnastics. For as long as she could remember, she had been number one in each of her age groups. The only people better than she was were always older and more experienced.

Looking around, Kelly saw some of the Gold Stars watching Maya. Several of them were talking among themselves and gesturing as though they were impressed.

As Maya calmly finished her straddles, Kelly suddenly realized that Maya was just as good as she was. For the first time Kelly knew she would have competition—competition from her own stepsister. Kelly wished she had tried harder on her straddle jumps instead of kidding around.

———————

When class was almost over, Kelly heard Dimitri clapping his hands loudly at the front of the gym.

"Attention, everyone!" he called. "Everyone gather around, please."

Kelly loved the way Dimitri talked. She thought he

sounded like a big bear. Monica gave her a little nudge, and they headed over to him with the rest of the Silver Stars.

"Listen up, everybody," Emma said once they were all gathered. "We have some exciting news. This year, for the first time, the Atlanta Strawberry Festival will be featuring a gymnastics competition. SGA, as well as four other gymnastics schools, will be competing."

"All right!" Kelly punched her fist in the air as the rest of the Silver Stars cheered.

"That's so cool," Monica said excitedly.

"Isn't that great, Maya?" Kelly said, still determined to make her stepsister feel part of things.

Maya nodded slowly. "My first American competition," she said. "I will have to work extra hard. I can't embarrass Papa or Emma."

Yeah. You sure don't want to end up having fun, Kelly thought in exasperation.

"Shhh, shhh," Dimitri said, waving his hands for quiet. "Let Emma speak!"

Emma gave him a warm smile, and he gazed back at her. Then she turned to the gathered students. "This is how it's going to work," she said. "There will be team competitions and some individual competitions. I'll choreograph the team competitions, but each team member will be responsible for his or her own routine for the individuals. Of course, Dimitri, Susan, and I will be glad to help anyone who asks. The Strawberry Festival is in two and a half weeks, so I need to see your routines no later than Thursday the thirteenth—that's nine days from now.

21

If you're not ready by then, you can't compete. We'll start rehearsals on the group routines by this Saturday. Are there any questions?"

One of the Copper Stars raised her hand. "Do we *have* to do things by ourselves?" she asked shyly.

Dimitri smiled, and his blue eyes twinkled. "No, Melanie," he said. "Students are not required to do the individual competitions."

Nodding, Emma said, "That's right. It's only if you want to."

"However," Dimitri said, "we encourage everyone to take part in the team routine. Each team needs five members to be eligible. If there are less than five, that team will be disqualified. Any other questions?"

One of the Gold Stars, Julie Stiller, raised her hand. "Are there awards?"

Kelly rolled her eyes meaningfully at Monica. "She *would* ask that," Kelly whispered softly. Julie was one of the very best Gold Stars—and one of the snobbiest. Kelly and her friends had nicknamed her Killer Stiller. But even though they didn't like Julie, they all wanted to be as good as she was. Last year, when Kelly had won the state championships for her age, Julie had won for hers too. Kelly knew Julie had her sights set on the Olympics. Though she was only fourteen, she had already competed in the Nationals, and once in Canada.

"Yes, there are awards," Emma answered. "There are individual medals and certificates, and there's one major prize for the group competition. The team that performs best will win five thousand dollars for their gymnastics school."

"Five thousand dollars!" Kelly gasped. "That's— that's—"

"Incredible," Monica said, finishing Kelly's sentence. "We could all get new team leotards and warm-up suits," she added excitedly. "Really hot ones!" When the Silver Stars competed in public, they wore identical leotards.

"We could get new equipment," Kelly pointed out. "Some of our mats are looking lame. And we could use another trampoline."

Harry tugged on Kelly's shoulder. "We could use the money to enter some out-of-state meets," she said, her dark eyes shining.

"It would be good for SGA to get the recognition," Maya said. "Then Papa and Emma would get even more students."

"That's right," Kelly said, pleased that Maya was getting caught up in the excitement. The possibilities swirled in Kelly's head. She motioned the other Silver Stars into a tight huddle.

"You guys," she said in a low voice, "we abso*tive*ly, poso*lute*ly have to win the Strawberry Festival team meet!"

Chapter Five

"Please pass the green beans," Kelly said at dinner that night.

Emma passed the bowl, and Kelly put some beans on her plate. "I'm totally excited about the Strawberry Festival," she said, smiling at her mother. "It's going to be so cool. You're going to give the Silver Stars an extra-special routine, right?"

Dimitri laughed. "Hold on, Kellinka. No favorites at SGA."

"What did you call me?" Kelly asked.

"Kellinka," Dimitri repeated. He smiled at her. "It's a Russian nickname for Kelly. But if you don't like it, I won't use it."

"Oh no," Kelly said, repeating it silently to herself. *Kellinka.* "I like it."

Clank. Maya's glass had knocked hard against her plate. "Sorry," she murmured.

"Are you excited about the meet too, Maya?" Emma asked.

"Yes," Maya answered. "It will be very interesting."

"It's going to be a lot of fun," Kelly said, stabbing a green bean and eating it. "I'm going to do the beam for the individuals. Please do something special for the group, Mom. Use cool music, or let us wear great costumes. Okay?"

"You heard Dimitri, young lady," Emma said, shaking her head. "We don't play favorites at SGA. You know that." She reached over to ruffle Kelly's hair. "But I hope you'll be happy with what I come up with."

———————

"What *is* this?" Monica asked the next day at lunchtime. Her delicate nose wrinkled.

Kelly examined the camouflage-colored glob on Monica's lunch tray. "Mystery meat, same as every Wednesday," she announced, putting an apple and a carton of milk on her own tray.

"Is that why you always bring your lunch on Wednesdays?" Monica asked, light dawning in her brown eyes.

"Yep." Kelly paid for her two things, then headed to their usual table. She didn't know how it had happened, but somehow the Silver Stars had started eating lunch together in the Sugarloaf Middle School cafeteria every day.

Harry and Maya were already at their table, which was in the middle of the last row by the windows. Harry waved her sandwich at Kelly in greeting.

"Have you worked out your individual routine yet?" she asked as Kelly sat down.

"Just a tiny bit," Kelly said. "I haven't thought the whole thing through, but I was thinking about it last night. It'll be the beam."

Harry nodded. "That's your best event," she agreed.

"Yeah." Kelly opened her insulated lunch bag and glanced across at what Maya was eating. "What is that—piroshki again?" Piroshki were little meat-filled dumplings. Dimitri had found them in the freezer section at the grocery store.

"Yes, piroshki," Maya said. "We were so glad to find them. I'm not used to all this rich American food." She looked around at their lunches, and so did Kelly. Kelly didn't see what kind of rich food Maya was talking about. They were all eating normal lunch-type stuff.

"Oh." Kelly couldn't think of anything else to say.

Monica came up and slid her tray next to Kelly's. "Ew! This lunch is so awful today! We might as well be in prison."

"I'm not positive, but I heard that the zoo is missing one of its elephants," Harry said seriously.

"Oh, no," Monica said, her eyes wide. Then she looked around and saw Kelly laughing behind her hand. "Oh. Very funny," she said sourly. "But it's *my* lunch you're laughing about."

"Sorry," Harry said cheerfully.

"What are you-all eating?" Monica asked, unwrapping her silverware.

Harry took a bite of sandwich. "Tuna fish."

"The usual," Kelly said, unwrapping her turkey sandwich on whole wheat with sprouts. She sighed and took a bite. Borriing.

"Maya?" Monica asked. Then she saw what Maya was eating. "Oh. The famous piroshki."

"They're very good," Maya said. She dipped one end into a little plastic container of sour cream. "Do you want to try one?"

Kelly and Monica made *ew* faces at each other. "No thanks," they both said at the same time.

"So, Monica," Harry said, "what about you? Have you decided on your individual routine yet?"

"Harry! It was announced only yesterday," Monica said, pushing her mystery meat around on her tray. She grimaced at it, then started in on her vegetables. "But I guess it'll probably be the vault."

"Maya and I have already talked about what we want to do," Harry said. She opened a plastic bag filled with apple and orange slices.

Kelly looked up. "You have?" Normally she was the only one on top of things. The others weren't usually as intense about gymnastics as she was.

Nodding, Harry shook her juice container. "Uh-huh. I hadn't really thought about it, but Maya is totally ready to go. That made me start thinking about it too."

27

"Really?" Kelly looked at Maya. "You didn't say anything last night at dinner. What event did you choose?"

"The beam," Maya said, shrugging her shoulders. "It's what I'm best at. I've won many medals."

Medals, huh? Kelly knew Maya was talented at gymnastics. Emma had told her so. And since Maya's arrival, Kelly had seen her stepsister's talent with her own eyes. But she hadn't known that the beam was Maya's specialty.

"Have you thought about exactly what you're going to do on the beam?" Kelly asked.

Maya nodded. "Just in my head. I'm going to start choreographing it this afternoon, after class," she said. "Papa will help me."

"Sure." Kelly nodded slowly. "I bet Mom would be glad to help too. She said she would help anybody who asked." Kelly took a sip of milk.

"It's kind of a drag we have to double up," Harry said, referring to the fact that since there were only four women's events—the beam, the uneven bars, the floor routine, and the vault—gymnasts from the same team often competed against each other. "I'm going to do the uneven bars, and I bet Kathryn is too."

"You're right, Harry," Kelly said. "But if we didn't double up, some of us wouldn't compete at all."

"Whoa," Candace said as she came up to the table and plopped her tray down hard. "Hey, y'all. What is this awful lunch?"

"Mystery meat," Monica said, pushing her tray away.

"I wish I could bring my lunch," Candace sighed, collapsing in her seat. "But I just can't get that organized. I figure if I get to school before first period starts, I'm doing okay."

"You could get up earlier," Harry suggested. Kelly knew that Candace's fluttering around got to Harry sometimes— she was so together herself, she couldn't understand someone who wasn't.

"Are you crazy?" Candace asked. Without waiting for an answer, she started digging into her food with gusto.

"Where's Kathryn?" Monica asked.

Rolling her eyes, Candace swallowed hard. "Probably in an Eggheads of America meeting. You won't believe this, but she missed last night's episode of *Kiss Yesterday Goodbye* just to study for today's French test."

"French test?" Monica shrieked. "Oops. I have a test in my French class too today."

Chapter Six

"Oh, Monica," Kelly said sympathetically. "Don't tell me you didn't study."

Monica dropped her head into her hands. "Oh, man," she moaned. "I completely forgot."

"French is your best subject," Kelly consoled her. "I bet you'll do fine, even without studying."

Monica whimpered.

"Sorry I'm late, guys," Kathryn said, putting down her lunch bag. "I got caught up in an extra-credit project."

"See?" Candace said to no one in particular.

"We were just talking about the Festival," Harry said.

"It'll be interesting to compete in my first American meet," Maya said. "I hope I'm prepared enough."

"Yeah," Kelly agreed. "Sometimes they can be kind of nerve-racking."

"Nerve-racking?" Maya frowned.

"Um . . ." Kelly thought for a minute. Maya spoke English really well, but sometimes she didn't know certain words. "Like, it makes you nervous," Kelly tried to explain. "Makes you tense, even if you feel confident."

"Oh." Maya nodded. "I was often nerve-racked when I performed in Russia. The judges there are very stern, and they would stare at me with hard eyes." She looked down at her empty lunch bag. "I had to do my very, very best. Really *had* to. It was always a relief when I placed first."

Always a relief when she placed first. Hmmm. So Maya didn't just win medals, she's used to winning first-*place medals,* Kelly thought as she took a bite of turkey sandwich. *Me too. If we both usually come in first, who's going to win when we compete against each other?*

"You should still try to do your very best here," Harry said, "only you don't have to get an ulcer about it or anything."

"But the competition can be really fierce," Monica pointed out. "At our last big statewide meet, I was so nervous, I thought I was going to throw up."

"I think I'll try a back somi dismount for the meet," Kelly said, crumpling up her sandwich bag. She had brought some graham crackers for dessert. "I was practicing it a lot at home with Mom last month." Kelly had seen the Gold Stars working on back flips off the beam without using their hands. It looked awesome. None of the other Silver Stars had tried a back somi yet. Kelly knew it was a hard move, but with more practice she felt she might be ready for it.

"That would be great," Monica said, nodding. "I bet Emma will let you try."

31

"Well, I'm going to ask Emma to help me choreograph a routine for the uneven bars," Harry said.

Kelly nodded. "You're great on the bars. Candace, what are you going to do?"

Candace took a sip of her juice. "No idea."

Kelly met Monica's eyes. Candace really liked gymnastics, and she was good at it, but Kelly thought Candace needed to take it more seriously.

"What about you, Kathryn?" Monica asked.

"The uneven bars, same as Harry." Kathryn smiled across the table at Harry, and Harry smiled back. "Let's just try not to do the exact same thing, okay?"

"Deal," Harry said.

"Listen, y'all," Kelly said, "what we really need to worry about is the group routine. We're going to be up against not only the other gymnastics schools, but teams from SGA, too."

"Does it matter which team wins?" Candace asked, finishing her dessert. "I mean, as long as it's a team from SGA?"

Kelly stared at Candace. "*Can*dace," she practically shrieked, "what do you mean, does it matter? Do you want the Gold Stars to win the team competition?" She felt as if her eyes were ready to pop out of her head.

Candace looked a little embarrassed. "Um, why not?" she asked mildly. "SGA will still get the money."

Monica shook her head. "I don't believe you," she said solemnly. "We don't want the *Gold* Stars to win."

"Although I guess we'd rather have the Gold Stars win

than have SGA not get the money at all," Kelly admitted. "But we really, really want the Silver Stars to place first. I mean, just think about it. The Gold Stars would practically drop dead of jealousy." She snickered, thinking about it.

"So we don't like the Gold Stars?" Candace asked.

Kelly sighed, remembering that Candace had been a Silver Star for only three weeks. "We can't stand them," she confirmed.

"Most of them are so stuck up," Monica complained. "Especially Julie Stiller."

"They act like we're total amateurs," Harry said.

"And they're not really that much better than us," Kathryn added. "Some of them know a few more things. But that doesn't give them the right to act so snobby."

"Okay." Candace nodded. "Got it. We don't like the Gold Stars."

"Right. So we, the Silvers, *have* to win the team competition," Kelly said firmly, shooting a glance at Maya. "No matter what."

Chapter Seven

"Do you like your bicycle?" Kelly called over to Maya the following Saturday morning. Since they lived only about ten blocks from SGA, Kelly often rode her bike to class. Last weekend, Dimitri, Emma, and Kelly had gone with Maya to pick out a bicycle for her. It was her very first.

Now, seeing Maya pumping the pedals of her shiny green mountain-style bike, Kelly thought that this was about the happiest she'd ever seen her new stepsister.

"Yes," Maya called back. "It's very efficient. And it's good exercise."

Turning her head so that Maya couldn't see, Kelly groaned to herself. What was wrong with Maya? Couldn't anything be plain old fun?

"Is school going okay?" Kelly tried again.

"Yes," Maya replied.

"How about SGA? Is it like your gym back home?"

They stopped for a traffic light. Maya seemed to be thinking. When they rode on again, she finally answered.

34

"No," she said. "It isn't much like the gym back home."

Kelly waited for Maya to explain, but her stepsister seemed to have said everything she wanted to say.

O-kaay, Kelly thought as she parked her bike outside of SGA. *I give up.*

———

In the girls' locker room, Kelly quickly changed from her school clothes into a leotard. With practiced movements, she pulled her shoulder-length brown hair into a tight ponytail and fastened it with a hair elastic. Pulling out a roll of white tape, she taped her palms from her wrist to her first knuckle. That, along with her palm guards, would help keep her calluses from ripping open. Then she was ready for class.

A few lockers down, Maya was doing the same thing. She was wearing a fresh black leotard and had pulled her hair back into a quick braid.

"Man, this is pathetic," said Monica.

Looking up, Kelly saw Monica standing at one end of the row of lockers, her hands on her hips, her backpack slung over one shoulder.

"What?" Kelly asked. "What's pathetic?" She looked around but didn't see anything.

"You two," Monica said firmly, walking to her own locker and dropping her backpack on the pink-painted bench. "I swear, if it wasn't for me, this place would have no style at all."

"What are you talking about?" Kelly asked.

"Look at you," Monica said, gesturing at Kelly while she took off her own school clothes. "You've been wearing that leotard since I've known you, and it wasn't new when we met." Monica had moved to Atlanta from New Orleans two years before.

Kelly looked down at her faded maroon long-sleeved leotard. "You're right," she sighed. "The worst thing is, I'm not even outgrowing it. It's going to wear out before it gets too small for me."

"You have a perfect build for gymnastics," Monica said loyally. "But look at me: I'm about to grow myself out of a gymnastics career." She pulled her T-shirt over her head. "And *you*, Maya. Black, black, black. It's like a funeral in here. You need some color." Monica stepped back and regarded Maya thoughtfully. "With your blond hair and blue eyes, you're a Summer. You should be wearing clear blues, greens, peaches."

"I should?" Maya looked down at her plain black leotard. Then she looked at Kelly's faded maroon one. "But I like dark colors."

"That's the problem. As for me—ta-daa!" Monica whirled around, her arms spread wide. She was wearing a sleeveless white unitard that ended above her knees. Swirls of neon red, neon blue, and sunburst pink were splashed across it. "See?" Monica said cheerfully. "This is *style*. You two have to get with the program."

"Get with what program?" Harry said as she came in and dumped her small duffel on the bench in front of her locker.

"The more-stylish-leotard program," Monica said, tying a floaty yellow chiffon scarf around her puffy dark ponytail.

"Oh," Harry said, taking off her shoes. "I thought you meant our group program. I bet Emma's come up with something fabulous. Did she tell you anything, Kelly?" Quickly Harry changed into a sleeveless, pale blue leotard and a matching pale blue scrunchie.

Kelly shook her head. "Nope. She never does. You know that."

"Hi, everyone," Kathryn said. She opened her locker and took out a short-sleeved lavender leotard and matching bike shorts. "I guess Candace isn't here yet."

Harry sniffed. "Big surprise. I don't know why Candace isn't more like you, Kathryn."

"We're fraternal twins, not identical," Kathryn said, stepping into her leotard. "Thank goodness."

"Okay," Emma said, standing by the large carpeted area under the windows. "While Susan works with the Gold Stars, I want to take you guys through your routine bit by bit. Then by the end of class, we'll put it all together."

Kelly and the rest of the Silver Stars were at the edge of the carpet with Emma. The carpet was short and dense, and made a large square, forty feet by forty feet, which was regulation size for the rhythmic gymnastics event. The Silver Stars were going to do rhythmic gymnastics for their group competition.

"Now, I've chosen a piece of music," Emma continued,

"and I've choreographed a routine using ribbons. You guys have used these before, at last year's spring recital." She held up several thin wooden dowels that had long, colorful ribbons attached.

Kelly grinned at Monica, and Monica grinned back. They had both loved using the ribbons last spring and had practiced with them since. And the year before, when they had watched the World Championships on TV, the rhythmic gymnastics routines using the ribbons had been one of their favorite events. Kelly could already see herself leaping around the carpet, making her long ribbon swirl and dance and twist through the air.

"We're also going to interweave more athletic elements into the routine." Emma smiled at them, then frowned. "Where's Candace?" she asked.

Automatically Kelly and the other Silvers glanced at Kathryn.

Kathryn shrugged, looking almost defensive. "She wasn't ready to leave with me and Mom, so I guess she had to take the bus."

Emma didn't say anything for a few moments, but Kelly could tell that her mother was irritated.

"Okay," Emma said, "I'll speak to her later. Now, the routine starts with two Silvers running out onto the carpets with their ribbons. We'll practice first without the music. The first two people are . . ."

Kelly immediately took a step forward. After all, she was the number-one Silver.

"Harry and Maya," Emma said.

Kelly stopped dead in surprise. Harry and Maya walked past her to the middle of the carpet, and Emma joined them. Slowly, not meeting anyone's eyes, Kelly slunk back to the edge. Her face was pink with embarrassment.

Monica touched her arm gently. "No one saw," she whispered.

Nodding, Kelly gave her a tiny smile. It was no big deal, she told herself. She was glad Harry was going to help lead the routine. But Maya? Maybe Emma had chosen Maya to help her feel more a part of the team. Still . . . Kelly couldn't help feeling upset.

Chapter Eight

"Too bad Maya didn't want to come," Harry said after class.

"Yeah—she wanted to hang out at SGA for a while, watching Dimitri," Kelly explained. Holding her cherry nut crunch cone, she followed Monica and Harry to a booth at the back of Gianelli's Ice Cream Shop. On the same old-fashioned strip mall where SGA was, there were several other stores, including Gianelli's. Kelly and the other Silver Stars loved to come here.

"And Candace and Kathryn had to go shopping with their mom," Monica reported. "I wonder what Emma said to Candace after class. She sure didn't look too happy that Candace was late again."

"Yeah. Candace better get with it," Kelly said.

"Is that 'Get with the stylish-leotard program,' or 'Get with the being-serious-about-gymnastics program'?" Harry teased.

Kelly and Monica laughed.

"Did you guys see Maya's back layouts?" Harry asked. "She's pretty amazing. They must train them super-hard in Russia."

"Um-hmm," Kelly said, pretending to concentrate on her ice cream. "Boy, this hits the spot."

"It hits *all* the spots," Monica corrected, licking her usual rocky road double cone.

"Thank heavens Gianelli's is practically right next door to SGA," Harry said. She stirred her orange sherbet with her spoon.

"Uh-huh. So! Our ribbon routine looks great," Monica said enthusiastically.

"Yeah. Emma did a good job of choreographing," Harry agreed. "I can't wait to practice it to music."

Without meaning to, Kelly sighed.

"What's the matter?" Monica asked, licking her cone to prevent drips.

"Well . . . I know this sounds stupid," Kelly said hesitantly. "And I guess it's selfish too."

"Uh-oh," Monica said. "Out with it."

"I just—I don't know. I guess I sort of wish Mom hadn't chosen Maya to start the routine," Kelly admitted.

"How come?" Harry asked.

"Oh, this is dumb," Kelly muttered, looking down at her cherry nut crunch cone. "It just seems that Maya's everywhere these days." She looked up and met her friends' eyes. "I mean, I like Maya fine. Or at least I'm trying to," she corrected herself. "But at home, she's in the room right next door to mine, playing that weird Russian pop music.

Or I go down to the kitchen, and she and Mom are having a cup of tea. And we have to share a bathroom. And she's at school, and she's at SGA. She's just everywhere."

"Well, it's a big change for you," Monica said. "And you're dealing with it a lot better than I would. So is Maya. You can't ask for more than that. It's only been two weeks."

"Yeah," Harry agreed. "Emma's probably just trying to make Maya feel at home."

"I guess," Kelly said, nodding. "Anyway, I feel better just telling you guys."

"That's what we're here for." Monica grinned.

"Hey, do y'all want to go to Schiffer's later?" Kelly asked, changing the subject. "I wanted to get some new palm guards."

"Oh my god," Monica gasped, clutching Kelly's wrist.

Kelly and Harry both stared at her.

"What's the big deal?" Kelly asked, tugging at her hand. "It's just new palm guards, for Pete's sake."

"No," Monica said in a low tone, her lips barely moving. "Over there. *There!* It's Beau Jarrett. He must be back from that meet in Canada."

Kelly and Harry immediately turned their heads to see.

"Don't look!" Monica screeched softly. "Don't look!"

"Monica, please," Kelly said in a matter-of-fact tone. "Get a grip. Beau Jarrett is a Gold Star. He's way too old for you."

"I know, I know," Monica moaned. "But he won't be forever. I mean, now he's sixteen and I'm twelve. But what about when he's twenty-five and I'm, um . . ."

"Twenty-one," Harry supplied.

"Right! It'll be perfect," Monica said.

Kelly grinned. "Don't hold your breath. Anyway, I think Mom mentioned that he has a girlfriend."

"Of course he does," Monica said, her dark eyes following Beau as he moved up in line. "He's gorgeous. That black hair, those green eyes . . . But that doesn't mean there's no hope for me in the future."

Harry rolled her eyes, and Kelly sighed.

"Oh, Beau, Beau," Kelly whispered dramatically, fluttering her hand over her heart. "Wherefore art thou, Beau . . ."

"You'll see," Monica muttered, not taking her eyes off Beau. "One day true love will come to you, and then you won't think it's so funny."

"Well, right now my only true love is gymnastics," Kelly said.

Monica frowned, ripping her eyes away from Beau and back to Kelly. "Mine too. I guess."

"Good. Now, don't get all moony." Kelly punched Monica's arm lightly. "We have a big meet coming up. I thought I'd start working on my solo routine today at home."

"It's going to be awesome," Harry said. "I've started to plan my program on the uneven bars. I need to smooth out my skin-the-cat."

"Oh, gosh, look—his favorite flavor is rocky road," Monica whispered. "This is it, y'all! It's fate!"

"Come on," Kelly muttered, trying to turn the key in her bike lock. It was getting rusty. She'd have to oil it soon. Harry and Monica had already left, and Kelly was on her way home too. Frustrated, she rattled the lock hard, then tried the key again.

"Okay, see you guys Monday," a voice called behind Kelly. She turned to see Julie Stiller, the talented and snobby Gold Star, waving to a couple of her teammates. When Julie spotted her, she seemed to hesitate, then came over to Kelly.

Great. Just what I need, Kelly thought. *A little chat with Killer Stiller.*

"Hi, Kelly," she said, hiking her gym bag higher on her shoulder.

"Hi, Julie," Kelly said. She put the key in the bike lock and turned it. It gave! With a little sigh of relief, Kelly unchained her bicycle.

"I was just watching your new stepsister in there." Julie motioned with her head back to SGA.

"Oh?" Kelly saw Maya's bike still in the rack.

"She was doing some moves with her dad. Wow, is she awesome," Julie said casually. "But I don't think she's ready to be a Gold Star."

Kelly frowned. "Of course not. She's only twelve years old."

"Tell *her* that," Julie said. "I heard her telling Dimitri she was tired of being on the baby squad. She says she needs more of a challenge."

Kelly felt her mouth drop open. "Maya didn't say that!"

44

Shrugging, as if she could care less what Maya had or hadn't said, Julie continued, "She did. Haven't you noticed how she's always bragging? 'In Russia everything was much harder,'" Julie mimicked. "'In Russia I always won. Things are so easy here.'"

Biting her lip, Kelly thought back to when Maya *had* said a few things like that.

"And you should hear what she says about *you*," Julie said, slanting her gaze on Kelly's face. "I can't believe you two are related now."

"What do you mean?" Kelly said. "What does she say about me?"

Julie shrugged again. "Just, you know, how she's so much better than you, and how you're so used to being number one, but you won't be number one for long. That kind of thing. That you're stuck up and full of yourself." Julie sounded as if she were discussing the weather.

Kelly's mind reeled in shock. She couldn't believe Maya would say those things about her. But why would Julie make it up? She'd practically never spoken to Kelly before —it wasn't as if they were enemies or anything.

"She's the one who's stuck up," Kelly said before she even realized it. "She doesn't want to be friends."

A tiny smile curled the edges of Julie's mouth. "I think so too," she said. "She thinks she's so much better than we are, just because she had Russian training."

"She's not any better than us!" Kelly cried.

"Nope," Julie agreed. "Oh, there's my ride. See you. And don't let Maya get you down."

Chapter Nine

"You've been awfully quiet tonight," Emma said, smoothing her hand over Kelly's hair. They had finished dinner, and Kelly was helping her mother load the dishwasher while Dimitri cleaned the kitchen.

"Yes, is everything okay, Kellinka?" Dimitri asked. "You went straight to your room when you got home."

"I'm fine," Kelly answered. But that wasn't true. All during dinner she had watched Maya carefully, looking for any sign that her stepsister had really said mean things about her to Julie. But Maya didn't seem different. *Maybe that's the problem,* Kelly had thought. *Maybe she's been this way from the beginning.*

Kelly put another plate in the dishwasher. Twice as many people, twice as many plates. "I guess I'll go downstairs and work on my routine," she said. "I'm still working out some of the choreography. Mom, in a little while, can you come down and help me with my back somi dismount?"

"Sure, honey," Emma said.

"A back somi dismount?" Maya walked into the kitchen wearing a warm-up suit over a black leotard. "I am going to use one too."

"What?" Kelly stared at Maya. "I told you at lunch the other day that I was going to try the back somi. Why didn't you say anything?"

Maya shook her head and shrugged. "It didn't seem important," she said. "I often used that dismount in Russia."

"You did?" It sounded as if she had mastered it, while Kelly was still working on it.

"Sure." Maya seemed unconcerned.

"There's no reason why both of you can't use the dismount," Dimitri said. "Kelly, with another week of practice, I'm sure you'll be comfortable with it."

Suddenly Kelly felt angry. "There's a big difference between being comfortable with it and having done it a bunch of times in competition," she said, her voice rising.

Maya stared at her. "Why are you upset?" she asked. "In Russia we often did the same things as each other."

"You're not in Russia anymore, Maya," Kelly snapped, "in case you haven't noticed." Throwing down her dishtowel, she flung open the basement door and stomped downstairs to their home gym.

"So then what happened?" Monica asked sympathetically on Monday afternoon. She and Kelly had gone to the Sug-

47

arloaf Mall after school, and now they were browsing through Schiffer's Sporting Goods store.

Kelly sighed. "I tried working on my routine, but I was too upset to do much. Then Mom came down and we talked about making Maya feel welcome, and how we were a family unit, blah, blah, blah."

"Did you tell her what was bothering you?"

"Not really. I didn't tell her what Julie said or anything." Kelly flipped through a rack of T-shirts.

"So what are you going to do?" Monica said, heading over to the exercise wear.

"Nothing, I guess. I mean, I *do* have to get along with her." Kelly made a face. "It just makes me so mad that she's been saying all that stuff—and to Julie. She still won't even talk to me, practically."

"Yeah," Monica agreed. "It's hard, 'cause we're all in the group routine together. Do you think Emma will show us the second half of our choreography tomorrow?"

"Yeah." Kelly nodded absently. "That's usually how Mom does it—one section at a time. Then we'll put the whole thing to the music."

"Hey, look at this two-piece exercise outfit," Monica said, pulling a hanger off a stand. "This is so cool. Do you think Emma would let me wear this to practice?"

Kelly put her head to one side, pretending to consider it. "Sure, why not?" she asked innocently. "I mean, just because your bare stomach would have all its skin scraped off the first time you did a kip on the uneven bars—still, that shouldn't stop you."

Monica looked at the outfit, then at Kelly. "Oh."

Laughing, Kelly shook her head. "There are reasons why we can wear only certain things."

"I guess," Monica muttered, putting the outfit back.

They walked over to a display of palm and hand guards. Kelly tried on the kind that she usually got and decided to get three sets. She went through palm guards quickly. There were also rolls of white athletic tape, and Kelly picked one up.

"So, what's Maya doing this afternoon?" Monica asked as they waited in line to pay.

"I think she probably went to SGA," Kelly said. "I thought I saw her riding her bike in that direction."

"What does she do when she isn't at the gym?" Monica asked.

Kelly opened her waist pack and took out her wallet. "I guess I don't really know," she admitted. "Why?"

Monica shrugged. "I just remember when I first moved to Atlanta two years ago, how nice you were to me, and how much that helped me feel like I fit in. I was wondering if Maya was having a really hard time. Maybe that's what's making her act superior."

"I don't know, Dr. Freud," Kelly said. "Maybe. Or maybe she's just not a very friendly person."

———

On Tuesday afternoon everything went wrong.

"Of course it's raining," Kelly complained to herself as she tried to unlock her bicycle from its rack outside school.

The rain pelted her, making her dark hair cling to her head like a wet blanket. Her polo shirt stuck to her damply, and she hoped it wasn't turning transparent.

She hadn't oiled her lock, and the rain was making it impossible to undo. She tried rattling it, and even pulled on the chain and hit the lock against the bike rack. Quickly she scanned the remaining bikes, but Maya's was already gone.

Finally she got her bike unlocked. Throwing her book bag in the front basket, Kelly hopped on and pushed herself off. SGA was eight long blocks away, but if she pedaled hard, she could get there in just a few minutes.

After about fifty feet, she noticed that her bike was dragging. She looked down.

"Oh, no!" she groaned. "Not my back tire!" Sure enough, it was flat. If she kept riding, the rim would bend, and then she'd have to replace the whole thing. She screeched to a halt, climbed off the bike, and started pushing.

Ten minutes later, when Kelly shoved her bike into the rack outside the gym, she didn't bother locking it—just looped the chain through the front wheel and hoped no one would be out stealing bikes in the rain.

Just as she got to the gym's glass double doors, a public bus pulled up to the corner. Candace jumped off, unfolding a bright yellow umbrella.

"Hi, Kelly!" she said cheerfully. "Whoa—you look like you lost a wrestling match with an alligator. Get stuck in the rain?"

"Yeah," Kelly said, pushing through the doors. "What

was your first clue?" She was drenched to the skin, covered with splashed mud up to her knees, and almost twenty minutes late. The last time she had been late was six months earlier, when an appointment at the dentist had taken longer than she had expected.

Inside, the Silver Stars had finished warming up and were working on their individual routines. Kelly looked for her mother so that she could explain about being late. She spotted Emma over by the beam. Maya was there too, and it looked as if she was doing . . .

Kelly's mouth thinned angrily as Maya put her hands in the air, pumped her arms down to get momentum, and did a back somi dismount off the beam. Emma and Susan Lu were spotting her on each side, but they hardly needed to touch her. Maya landed a little shakily but didn't fall over.

"Great!" Emma said, giving Maya a big smile. Maya nodded and gave a tiny smile back.

Kelly blinked. Even after she had told her mother how upset she was by Maya's doing the back somi, here she was helping Maya. It was so disloyal. Emma knew how much Kelly had wanted to get it perfect in time for the competition. And here was her very own stepsister, stealing Kelly's idea. The really awful thing was, Maya was actually better at the back somi than Kelly.

Chapter Ten

For a long moment Kelly just stood there, chilled and dripping wet, her teeth clenched. Then she became aware of someone looking at her. Turning, she saw Killer Stiller over by the floor mats. Julie made a sympathetic face and shrugged as if to say "I told you so."

Kelly looked away. Harry had started practicing her routine on the uneven bars, and Emma was now spotting her. Then Emma saw Kelly and Candace standing just inside the doors. Her face creased in a frown, and she told Harry to take a break.

Kelly waited for her mother to come over and ask if she was all right, ask why she was soaking wet and covered with mud, ask if she wanted a nice hot cup of tea.

"Kelly, Candace," Emma said. She looked pointedly at her watch. "Class started at three-thirty. You are both more than twenty minutes late."

"But, Emma," Kelly began, shocked that her mother

was obviously blaming her for something that wasn't all her fault.

"One minute, Kelly." Emma raised her hand for silence. "I know you're usually on time, but today, when you realized you were going to be late, you should have called. And Candace, I've warned you about your chronic tardiness before. If you can't take gymnastics more seriously, perhaps you should consider another sport. Because you were both late, your team couldn't begin to learn the second half of the group choreography. You've let them down. Now get changed and warmed up as quickly as possible. Let's see if we can salvage what's left of the afternoon."

While Kelly gaped after her, Emma turned and strode back to Harry on the uneven parallel bars.

This is so unfair! Kelly thought miserably, heading for the girls' bathroom.

"Whoa," Candace chuckled, walking beside her. "Emma seemed really rattled. Guess she woke up on the wrong side of the bed this morning." She whistled tunelessly as they walked the length of the gym to the back.

Kelly gritted her teeth. "Emma's mad because we're late," she said pointedly. "Everyone else got here on time. Aren't you even a little upset that she suggested you find another sport?"

"Oh, she didn't mean it," Candace said cheerfully. "Teachers always get bent out of shape if you're different. But I'm really good at gymnastics—I mean, I'm already a Silver Star. Emma's probably just having a bad day. I'm not worried." With a jaunty wave, she headed into the locker room to change as Kelly went into the bathroom to wash the mud off.

Maybe you should *be worried,* Kelly thought sourly. No matter what Candace believed, Kelly knew that her mother would never have said such a thing if she hadn't been dead serious. If Candace didn't watch out, she was going to find herself a Twinkler. *And what about me?* Kelly wondered as she quickly washed off the worst of the mud. *I should be worried too. Next thing you know, Maya's going to be wearing my clothes and sleeping in my bed.* Kelly's jaw set grimly. Nobody said she had to take it lying down.

———

"Now, I want everyone to do a front pike somersault," Emma said twenty minutes later.

Kelly stood with the rest of the Silver Stars on the carpet. She was trying to look extra attentive to make up for being late. She wanted to show her mother that she was just as good as Maya at everything. It had been really hard to swallow her anger, but Kelly knew this wasn't the time or the place for confrontations. One of the hardest things she had learned about being a gymnast was that sometimes you had to put your feelings in a little locked box so that you could concentrate on your performance. After the performance, you could unlock the box. But not during. Now she watched Emma carefully to learn the routine.

"Then up into a standing position," Emma continued. "Harry, Candace, and Monica will do a half pivot so that you're facing Kelly, Kathryn, and Maya. Then the six of you will do simultaneous front walkovers, so that you mesh, like this."

Emma bustled around, moving the Silver Stars into position as she spoke so that they would understand where they were supposed to be in relation to each other.

"After you-all do this section, you'll end up in a line, with Kathryn at the head. Then you'll take your ribbons and—"

"Excuse me, Emma?" Candace raised her hand. "I'm thirsty. Can we take a break?"

Emma glanced at her watch. "Candace, we took a break fifteen minutes ago. Didn't you have water then?"

Candace shook her head. "I wasn't thirsty before."

Emma looked at her silently.

Kelly, who knew that look all too well, practically shivered.

Just as silently, Emma motioned for Candace to get a drink of water. With a smile, Candace ran over to the water fountain.

"If I were her, I'd rather die of thirst than have Mom look at me like that," Kelly whispered to Monica.

"And on top of being late too," Monica whispered back.

"We'll continue without Candace," Emma said calmly. "Now, I want one single line, facing the back of the gym."

———

"I'm starving," Monica said in the locker room after class. "I hope dinner's ready when I get home."

"Whose turn is it to cook?" Kelly asked. She looked around for Maya, but her stepsister hadn't come into the locker room yet.

"Dad's," Monica said happily.

Kelly couldn't help grinning. All the Silver Stars knew that Monica's mom, who was a police detective, was an awful cook.

Humming to herself, Candace changed quickly into her street clothes. As she stood in front of the mirror, brushing her hair, Harry met Kelly's eyes. Her look said, *Say something.*

Kelly felt uncomfortable. It wasn't her job to make Candace be more responsible. She wasn't the teacher. On the other hand, Candace was headed for trouble at SGA, and as a friend, Kelly ought to warn her about it.

"Um, Candace . . . ," Kelly began, trying to sound casual. "It was a drag getting yelled at by Emma, huh?"

"She's probably used to it," Kathryn said sourly, brushing out her dark red hair.

Kelly tried again. "I'm sure going to try not to be late again," she said.

Candace patted her bright red, shoulder-length curls. "Oh, I bet her bark is worse than her bite," she said breezily.

Monica looked up in alarm. "Oh, no, Candace," she said, tying her hiking-boot laces. "Her bark isn't half as bad as her bite. Take it from me. Last year Emma actually asked a kid to leave and not come back. You guys remember that? She was a Bronze Star."

Kelly and Harry nodded solemnly.

"You should be more careful, Candace," Kathryn said briskly. "Emma takes gymnastics very seriously. And so do we."

"Kathryn's right," Kelly said.

Turning around, Candace faced them with a patient look on her face. "Guys," she began, "I really don't think you need to worry about me. Quit being so serious all the time. Okay?" She picked up her tote bag and left the locker room.

Just as Kelly was about to say something, Maya walked in, followed by Julie Stiller and two other Gold Stars. Maya was biting her lip, and her face looked pinched and upset. For just a moment, her blue eyes met Kelly's, and Kelly was surprised to see that she looked hurt. Or maybe she was angry.

What has she got to be angry about? Kelly thought. *She's the one going around saying awful things about me.*

"Hi, kids," Julie said, heading for her locker. "Maya, I saw you working on your back somi dismount. Looked good."

Maya only nodded and sat down on the bench to pull on her socks. Kelly could feel Maya looking at her again but refused to meet her eyes.

Turning her back on Maya, Julie caught Kelly's attention. "Are you going to let her steal your routine?" she mouthed silently.

Kelly didn't respond. But inside she knew that she was going to have it out with Maya—and soon.

Chapter Eleven

"Kelly, could you set the table, please?" Dimitri asked in his deep, gravelly voice.

"Okay," Kelly said unenthusiastically. She slowly got up from where she was doing her homework on the living room floor and headed to the kitchen. Since they had gotten home from SGA, she and Maya had been avoiding each other.

How dare Maya act like I've *done something to* her? Kelly fumed silently. *I'm the wronged one here.*

In the kitchen, Emma was bending over to look in the oven. The yummy smell of baking chicken wafted through the room. Maya was in front of the microwave, taking a casserole out. She looked solemn, almost sad. When Kelly came into the room, Maya's jaw clenched.

"I think the vegetables are ready, Emma," Maya said quietly.

Suddenly it was all too much for Kelly. Maya had said mean things about her, had stolen her beam dismount, and now she was worming her way into Emma's heart—being the little kitchen helper. "Doesn't this look cozy," Kelly said tightly.

Her mother turned at the sound of Kelly's voice. "What?"

"This." Kelly waved her arms around the kitchen, including Dimitri, who was getting plates out of a cupboard. "We're just one big happy family. The four of us."

Kelly saw her mother look at her in surprise and saw Dimitri look at Emma, as if she could explain to him what was happening.

Slowly Maya put the vegetable dish down on the counter. "You're mad at me, aren't you?"

"You bet I am. You think you're so great, doing the back somi dismount," Kelly said. "You're so stuck up, you won't even be friends with me and the other Silver Stars. And today, I get to the gym after getting caught in the rain with a flat bicycle tire, and there you are, showing off in front of everyone, acting like you're better than me."

Maya's blue eyes flashed angrily. "I wasn't showing off," she snapped. "I can't help it if I'm more advanced at gymnastics than you. Maybe I'm used to working harder! Maybe I don't get everything handed to me because everyone thinks I'm so great! You're just a spoiled American!"

Kelly's mouth dropped open. "Whaat?" she shrieked.

Stepping between them, Emma held up her hands for silence. "That's enough, girls," she said firmly. "You're both obviously upset about a number of things. But right now I want you to shelve your differences. Let's sit down and eat, and after dinner we'll try to work out what's bothering you."

"Kellinka, I didn't know your bicycle tire was flat," Dimitri said. "If you help me, I think we can fix it tomorrow."

"Don't bother!" Kelly shouted. "Who cares about my stupid bicycle tire? Who cares about anything I do?" Then, feeling as though she was about to burst into tears, she ran upstairs to her room and slammed the door.

Chapter Twelve

"Hold me forever, never let me go . . ." The mournful voice of the lead singer of Kelly's favorite band, Skyrocket, floated through her room, bringing a lump to her throat. Kelly was lying on her bed with her feet up on the wall, right at the bottom of her Nadia Comaneci poster. Had Nadia ever had problems like this? She probably had, Kelly acknowledged. Or if not exactly like this, then other big problems that she'd had to overcome.

Looking at Nadia cheered Kelly up a bit. Like Kelly, Nadia had been small for her age and tightly muscled. Like Kelly, she had taken her gymnastics seriously.

"Someday I'll be as good as Nadia," Kelly vowed. She threw one of her pillows against the wall. "No matter what Maya does."

A gentle tap on her door made Kelly jump.

"Kelly, honey? May I come in?" Emma sounded concerned.

"I guess," Kelly said.

When Emma came in, her face looked worried. Her wavy, dark brown hair had been pushed carelessly off her forehead. Kelly slid over on her bed to make room.

Emma sat beside her. Kelly waited. Was her mother going to yell at her? Make her apologize?

"Our lives have changed a lot in the past month," Emma said finally.

"Uh-huh."

"For the first time in your life, you have to share me with other people at home," Kelly's mother continued.

"Yeah." Kelly felt surprised. She hadn't thought her mother knew what she was going through.

"Not only that, but your very own stepsister is a great gymnast," Emma said.

Frowning, Kelly leaned back and looked at her poster again. Hearing Emma say that Maya was great made her heart hurt.

"For the first time, there's someone your age who's as good as you are, as serious as you are about gymnastics. That must be really hard for you."

Suddenly Kelly felt close to tears again. She nodded and rubbed her hand across her eyes.

Emma reached out and smoothed Kelly's hair. "It's not just the back somi, is it?"

"No," Kelly muttered in a wavery voice. "Maya just—I mean, I've tried to like her. I really have. But she isn't friendly. She doesn't like me or my friends. All she does is gymnastics, and now she's doing my routine. And she's—"

Kelly was about to tell Emma all the mean things Maya had been saying about her, but something held her back. She didn't want Emma to worry about how bad things had gotten between them. After a long time alone, Emma was happy with Dimitri. Kelly didn't want to ruin that.

"Nothing," Kelly said, sniffling. "I guess we're just not used to each other."

"Hmmm." Emma looked thoughtful. "You know, you and Maya are really quite different, although you're both terrific at gymnastics. I bet your solo routines will be very different too, even if you both have the back somi as your dismount. I tell you what: Let's work really hard on the back somi together over the next few days. And if it's ready, use it in the meet. It doesn't matter what Maya's doing."

"Really?" Kelly asked. "But she does it better than me."

"Kelly. You're a fabulous natural gymnast. I'm sure if you work at the move, you'll master it soon. It's a question of—"

"Mind over matter," Kelly finished.

Laughing, Emma reached down and hugged her daughter. "You know me too well," she said. "Now, about your fight with Maya . . ."

Kelly waited for her mom to say they had to make up and love each other and be good stepsisters.

"I think you two need to give each other some time and some space," Emma said, surprising Kelly again. "You're going through some huge changes in your life, and so is she. At least you still have your same school and your same friends. She has only Dimitri here—everything else is brand-new. So cut her some slack, and try to stay out of each other's way for a while. Okay?"

"Okay," Kelly agreed. Staying out of Maya's way definitely sounded good right then.

"And maybe in the future—who knows? You might end up liking each other." Emma patted Kelly's shoulder. "Stranger things have happened."

"Maybe," Kelly said politely. *And maybe not.*

It was actually easy not to talk to Maya, especially since Maya seemed to be going out of her way to avoid Kelly too. On Wednesday morning, Kelly waited until Maya had come out of the bathroom they shared. Then she went in and locked the door. When she was ready for school, Kelly didn't wait for Maya, as she usually did. She just grabbed her book bag and ran out of the house.

At school they had only three classes together: homeroom, because their last names both started with *R;* English in third period; and math in sixth period after lunch.

In homeroom Kelly pretended to be busy finishing up her history homework. Maya didn't even look at her.

During English, their teacher, Ms. McKenzie, gave them an assignment for a one-page paper due at the end of class. The topic: friendship.

Bending low over her desk, Kelly took the top off her pen and started to write. "Friendship means you have to be nice to the other person. You have to smile sometimes and talk to them and make an effort. And it means loyalty above all," she wrote in big, dark script. "Like, if you're planning to do a special dismount for your routine, a true friend would never steal your idea. Not even if your mom said it was okay."

The bell rang just as Kelly was finishing up.

Lunchtime was harder, because they all usually sat together. If Kelly hadn't been too distracted to make her lunch that morning, she could have met Monica and asked to sit with her at some other table. But while Kelly was waiting in the lunch line, Monica came in and sat with Candace at their usual table. Harry was moving through the crowd toward them, and Maya was right behind her.

Well, I'll sit there, Kelly reasoned to herself. *She's not going to drive me away from my friends. But I'm still not talking to her.*

The hot lunch was mystery meat as usual, which seemed to fit her mood. Kelly paid for her lunch, took her tray, and headed for her table.

Maya didn't even look up when Kelly sat down. She had bought the hot lunch too, Kelly noticed.

"Hey, y'all," Kelly said smoothly as she pulled out her chair and sat down.

"I got a B on that French test I didn't study for," Monica said.

"Great," Candace said, blowing a few bubbles into her milk. "Never let 'em see you sweat."

Out of the corner of her eye, Kelly could see Maya look a little startled. She probably hadn't understood the American expression. Well, Kelly wasn't going to explain it.

Monica sat forward, unwrapping her cookie. "So I've been working on my vault routine. I'm going to go with the front handspring with a full twist."

Kelly gave a genuine smile. "That's great, Monica. I'm sure you'll do really well."

"Thanks." Monica took a bite of cookie. "So, are we all going to wear matching uniforms to the Strawberry Festival?"

Harry nodded. "Of course. But which ones?"

"What are our choices?" Candace asked. Since she'd been a Silver Star for only four weeks, she'd never competed in public with them before.

"Um . . . there are white ones with gold trim," Monica said, "navy blue ones with a silver star on them, and pale green ones with white trim all down the sleeves."

"The white ones with gold trim are probably a little old," Kelly said. "We wore those last year a lot."

"This is really exciting," Candace said, bouncing in her seat a little. "My first public performance."

"Have you decided what you're doing yet?" Monica asked.

Candace nodded. "I'm going to do the vault, same as you." She smiled.

Glancing quickly across the table, Kelly saw Monica's eyes widen. Her sandwich was halfway to her mouth, but Monica let it hang in midair.

66

"Really?" Monica said. "I thought you'd go for a floor routine or something."

Candace waved her hand dismissively. "I thought about it, but then on Saturday when I saw you doing the vault, you made it look so neat. It made me want to do it too."

"Oh." Monica nodded slowly, looking at the table. Then she shrugged. "We have to show our routines to Emma tomorrow. Do you think you'll be ready by then?"

Nodding, Candace opened a bag of chips. "Sure. I always work best under pressure. Anyone want a chip?"

Kelly took a chip and crunched it thoughtfully. *If Candace has a routine together by tomorrow,* she thought, *I'll eat my palm guards.*

Chapter
Thirteen

"How was school today?" Emma asked. "No, put your feet a tiny bit apart, one after the other."

On Wednesday night after dinner, Kelly and her mom had taken over the basement workout room. Maya and Dimitri had stayed upstairs, where they were going over Maya's homework. Now Emma was helping Kelly with her back somi.

The balance beam at home was only two feet off the ground, so Kelly had to depend on Emma's help in the actual landing.

"It was okay. Maya and I are staying out of each other's way." Kelly adjusted her feet on the beam, feeling the four-inch-wide band of wood beneath her toes. "Ready?"

"Yep." Emma positioned herself. "Go."

Coiling her body down, Kelly threw herself backward as though she were doing a very tight back handspring. She felt her body turning upside down but concentrated on getting her knees under her fast. Then her mother's hands —one on her back, one on her stomach—helped flip her the rest of the way. Quickly Kelly straightened out her legs, and her feet hit the foam mat.

"Excellent!" Emma said. "You're definitely getting the height and the speed you need. I think on a regulation beam you would have nailed the landing."

Kelly smiled. "Really?"

"Yes. It's much better than it was a month ago. You've worked hard on it." Emma rubbed Kelly's back gently.

"Thanks." A warm glow started in Kelly's stomach and spread throughout her limbs. It made her feel good to know that she would soon be as polished as Maya at the dismount. She was holding her own. Kelly was going to stay number one, and the sooner Maya accepted that, the better.

"Can we do it a couple more times?" Kelly asked.

"Sure," Emma said.

———

"There he goes, there he goes," Monica whispered to Kelly on Thursday afternoon at SGA.

Kelly looked up to see Beau Jarrett crossing over to the men's even parallel bars.

"Oh, gosh, my heart is beating so hard, I might faint," Kelly said in a fluttery voice. She blinked rapidly and patted her chest.

"Very funny," Monica said, sliding into a straddle split on the floor. She pointed her toes and slowly stretched out, rubbing the backs of her knees to help loosen the muscles.

"He's got to notice you today," Kelly said reassuringly. "I mean, look at what you've got on."

Monica looked at herself in the wall mirror. "What?"

Laughing, Kelly shook her head and got down on the floor to stretch beside Monica. Maybe Monica didn't see anything unusual about a bright yellow sleeveless leotard, bright green leg warmers, and a fluorescent yellow and green headband, but Kelly thought they stood out.

"Hey, if I'm at one end of the clothes spectrum," Monica said, "you're at the other. Seriously—we have *got* to take you shopping."

Kelly nodded sheepishly. "You're right. I guess I am ready for a new look. We can go after the Strawberry Festival."

Monica was about to reply when Susan Lu clapped her hands over by the floor carpet. "Silver Stars, over here! Let's line up and see your individual routines!"

She and Dimitri were holding clipboards, and Kelly knew they would judge the Silver Stars' routines and suggest improvements if necessary. Kelly jumped to her feet and followed Monica over to the carpet. After working with her mother on the dismount at home, Kelly felt confident enough to try it here.

She was also curious about everyone else's routines. Maya had been warming up with Harry, and Candace had been standing with Kathryn, chatting to her while Kathryn stretched.

Be professional, Kelly Elizabeth Reynolds, Kelly told herself firmly. *Don't let your feelings get in the way. They're in a locked box, remember?* Standing tall, Kelly straightened her shoulders. Today she was going to do the best routine she could—with a back somi. If she messed up, and Susan and Dimitri didn't qualify her for the meet, then she would go to Plan B: a roundoff dismount. *That* she knew she was good at.

"Okay, first, Harry on the uneven parallel bars," Susan said, consulting her clipboard.

The Silver Stars trooped over to the bars.

After dipping her hands in chalk, Harry walked lightly over the mats to the uneven bars. Then she did a front hip pullover onto the low bar and went into her routine. Susan and Dimitri stood on each side of the bars, spotting her.

First Harry did a glide swing on the low bar, then a straddle swing. On her next time around, she pulled her feet up so that she was crouching on the low bar; then she sprang and grabbed the high bar. Pulling herself up with a kip, she did another front hip pullover, then went into one of her hardest moves: a clear hip circle to a handstand. When Harry was steadying her handstand on the high bar for a few seconds, Kelly held her breath. She had learned that move last year and knew that it was hard and even a little scary at first.

"Wow," Candace said softly, watching her. "She's really great. I hope I can do that someday."

You won't if you don't get more serious, Kelly thought. She felt keyed up and nervous, the way she usually did before an exhibition.

Then Harry did a skin-the-cat and dropped down to the low bar for another straddle swing. A simple back flip was her dismount.

Landing squarely on both feet, Harry shot her arms up

in the "touchdown" position that all gymnasts use at the end of a routine.

Kelly and the other Silver Stars clapped hard.

"Very good, Harry," Susan said, writing something on her clipboard. "That'll be a terrific routine for the Strawberry Festival." Harry looked pleased.

"It almost makes me wish I had chosen the uneven bars," Candace whispered.

"You wish!" Kathryn said with disbelief. "You have a couple years of practice before you'll be able to do that."

Candace stuck her tongue out at her sister.

After Harry, Monica did her vault routine, which consisted of three different jumps. The first jump was a simple straddle, but Monica achieved tremendous height and had perfect form. Kelly gave her a big thumbs-up when Monica trotted down the mat for her second jump.

Kelly and the other Silver Stars watched as Monica ran down the mats, bounced off the springboard in front of the vault, and did a handstand on the vault. Then her body curled over and she landed perfectly on the mat.

"Very nice, Monica," Susan said.

"Are you sure about your third vault—the front handspring into a full turn?" Dimitri asked.

"Yes, I'm sure." Monica nodded. Then she went to the beginning of the mats again.

Even from almost forty feet away, Kelly could see Monica's brow wrinkle with concentration. Her eyes narrowed, her body tensed. Kelly held her breath in anticipation.

Chapter Fourteen

Monica started running down the length of the mats, arms pumping at her sides. She jumped onto the springboard, bounced high, and landed in a handspring on top of the vault. Then she flew high through the air, twisting vertically, her arms flat and tucked at her sides. Her legs were straight, her toes pointed, and her puffy, dark brown ponytail was sailing behind her like a cloud. She landed on the mat, facing the opposite direction she had started in. But she didn't land completely straight, so her legs buckled a bit and she wobbled. Susan and Dimitri grabbed her waist, but Monica was already straightening up by herself, her arms held high overhead, a huge smile lighting her face.

"All right!" Kelly yelled, clapping hard.

"Wonderful, Monica," Susan said, patting Monica's shoulder. "Just terrific."

"We'll work on that landing," said Dimitri, but he was smiling.

Monica came back to the line of Silver Stars, and Kelly gave her a high five. "That was fabulous. I can't wait to see you do that at the Strawberry Festival."

"Thanks," Monica said with a grin.

"Totally awesome," Harry said. "The vault is definitely your event."

"In Russia we have a saying for someone who is very graceful and strong," Maya said. "We say, 'You looked like a bird. Like a, um . . .'" she searched for the word. "A falcon? Right? Just now, you looked like a falcon."

"Thanks, Maya," Monica said. She gave Kelly a glance.

Now what is Maya doing? Kelly thought. *Trying to steal my best friend?*

Next was Maya's routine on the beam. Kelly didn't want to watch, but she had to. They all moved over to the regulation-height beam, and Susan and Dimitri stood on each side.

Okay, Ms. Know-it-all, Kelly thought. *Let's see your stuff.*

First Maya bounced off the springboard into a simple side-squat mount. She went into a no-hands straddle split on the beam, keeping her toes pointed and her hands and wrists in a flexed position. Bringing her legs together, she moved into a very slow and controlled handstand.

Ugh. That looks great, Kelly thought sourly. *I wish I had thought of that.*

From the handstand Maya lowered her head to one side of the beam and did a simple tucked somersault, and then slid right into a standing position. After that came two front handsprings, and then she was poised on the beam for her dismount.

Kelly watched Maya intently. Her hands curled into fists. This was *her* dismount. The one Maya had done many times back in Russia.

Maya coiled down, then sprang backward, curling through the air above everyone's heads. Susan and Dimitri automatically moved forward to help her land, if necessary.

But Maya landed smoothly and in control, her feet planting themselves firmly on the mat. With a smile, she straightened up and threw her arms over her head.

Great, Kelly thought bitterly. *Just great.*

"That was terrific, Maya," Susan said, marking it down on her clipboard. "Very well done."

"Good, sweetheart," Dimitri said, ruffling Maya's hair.

"Way to go, Maya," Candace said.

Kelly didn't say anything. As Maya stepped off the mat, she sent a chilling look in Kelly's direction. Kelly frowned.

"I'll go next," Kathryn offered. "It's the uneven bars again."

Kathryn began by bouncing off a springboard and grabbing the high bar. Then she pulled herself up into a kip and did a free hip swing. After gathering momentum, she let go of the high bar and flew toward the low bar, touching it with her stomach right before she grabbed it with both hands. From there she did a monkey swing, releasing one hand to do a half turn. After a straddle swing, she ended by doing a forward somersault from a hanging position off the high bar.

"Excellent!" Dimitri boomed, giving Kathryn a quick hug.

"That was beautiful, Kathryn," Susan said, writing on her clipboard.

Kathryn came over to the other Silver Stars, wearing a self-conscious smile of satisfaction.

"That was terrific, Kathryn," Kelly said. "Good for you."

"Thanks," Kathryn said, wiping her face with a clean white gym towel.

"Awesome," said Harry.

Kathryn laughed, looking pleased and embarrassed at the same time.

"Okay, now me, me, okay?" Candace said, bouncing a little on her toes. "It's my turn."

"All right, Candace," Susan said, finishing writing Kathryn's report. "You're going to do the vault, right?"

"Right," Candace said, hurrying over to the same vault that Monica had used. "First I'll do a straddle jump, like Monica, then a forward somersault, then a handspring."

Susan looked concerned. "Candace, have you practiced the forward somersault and the handspring enough? Those are difficult moves."

Candace brushed a strand of red hair out of her face. "No prob," she said breezily. "Piece of cake."

"Have you warmed up enough?" Susan persisted. "You must be very loose and flexible for the straddle jump."

"Of course I warmed up," Candace said indignantly. She headed down to the end of the mats.

"Did she warm up?" Monica whispered to Kelly.

76

"I didn't see her," Kelly whispered back.

"I'm worried about her," Kathryn said softly, leaning over Kelly's shoulder. "She mostly just talked to me while *I* warmed up. She doesn't think anything takes practice."

The Silver Stars stood in a silent row as Candace began to run down the line of mats.

Just as Monica had done, Candace bounced hard off the springboard in front of the vault. Instantly Kelly could see that Candace had bounced *too* hard. The red-haired girl was barely able to brush her fingertips against the top of the vault before she flew over it awkwardly, high in the air. Susan and Dimitri grabbed at her, but she slipped through their hands. Candace was so surprised, she forgot to bring her feet together for the landing, and instead crash-landed face-first on the deep cushion of the mats.

Chapter Fifteen

Susan and Dimitri rushed over to Candace.

"Candace! Are you all right?" Susan asked anxiously, examining Candace's hands and wrists. "Answer me, please."

"Yeah, I'm okay," Candace said. Her voice sounded shaky.

When Susan realized that Candace was only shaken up, her face took on a serious look. "You obviously have not prepared that element sufficiently," she said, retrieving her clipboard from the floor and writing something next to Candace's name. "What about the somersault and the handspring?"

Candace looked uncertain for a moment; then Kelly saw her natural bravado take over.

"I just miscalculated a little, that's all," she said. "I know I can do the somersault and the handspring."

Dimitri and Susan exchanged a glance. From where she

stood on the sidelines, Kelly knew what that glance meant: They knew Candace wasn't ready.

Gently, Dimitri put his hand on Candace's shoulder. "You have a lot of natural talent, Candace," he said in his deep voice. "If you worked hard, you could do great things with gymnastics. But you do not work hard. Emma and I have spoken to you about this. And now, today, you endangered yourself by attempting elements for which you are not ready."

"You could have broken something," Susan said sternly. "Is that what you want? To break your wrist or your ankle?"

Biting her lip, Candace hung her head. "No," she said in a small voice.

Kelly couldn't help feeling sympathetic. She knew that Candace had no business doing fancy moves, but at the same time, it must be humiliating to be scolded in front of everyone. Glancing around, Kelly saw that the rest of the Silver Stars looked uncomfortable. A few other students had stopped to listen too. Melanie Lyons, a Copper Star, was watching with wide eyes. A couple of Gold Stars were hiding smiles behind their hands. Julie Stiller was frowning and shaking her head.

Susan sighed. "Candace, did you really and truly warm up and practice your routine thoroughly?"

Candace hesitated, playing with a strand of her hair. Finally she took a deep breath. "No," she admitted.

Kelly was silent, waiting with the other Silver Stars to see what would happen. Susan and Dimitri exchanged glances again; then Dimitri sighed and ran a hand through his short blond curls.

"Okay," he said in his accented English. "I'll speak to Emma about this. But you may not compete in the individual routines at the Strawberry Festival."

"What?" Candace gasped, staring from Susan to Dimitri. Then she laughed shakily. "Okay, I get it," she said, nodding. "You're teaching me a lesson. Now I know. Okay. I'll practice really hard, and show you my routine on Saturday. How's that?"

Kelly glanced over at Monica, Harry, and Kathryn. They all looked a little depressed. Maya was expressionless.

"She doesn't get it," Monica whispered in Kelly's ear.

Kelly grimaced. "She will soon," she predicted glumly. As much as she wanted Candace to be more serious about gymnastics, she knew how disappointing it would be not to be able to compete in the solos.

Susan shook her head. "I'm sorry, Candace," she said gently. "Everyone had to have their routine in good shape by today. It wasn't an option, it was a requirement. You can speak to Emma about it, but Dimitri and I are not qualifying you to compete."

Candace's jaw dropped open. "Oh, come on," she said, sounding a little angry. "I said I'd work extra hard over the next few days."

"We won't bend the rules for you, Candace," Dimitri said firmly. "The sooner you begin to act more responsibly, the better off you'll be. Now you can start by accepting our decision, and accepting your part in it. Of course, you can still be in the group routine."

Her face flushing with anger and embarrassment, Candace looked around at the Silver Stars. Kelly met her eyes and tried to send her a sympathetic glance.

"I told you," Kathryn said to her sister. "You wouldn't listen."

Candace's face hardened. "You guys are all stupid!" she cried. "You act like gymnastics is the only thing in the world! Well, I know better, and I'm not going to waste my time anymore." Then she spun on her heel and stomped off toward the girls' locker room.

Kathryn sighed, looking after her twin. "I was hoping she would get her act together," she said. "But she's done the same thing with horseback riding, and karate, and piano lessons . . ."

Susan clapped her hands. "Okay, it's Candace's choice. Let's move on, people. We need to see Kelly's routine before we go on to practicing the group event."

Chapter Sixteen

"Will you please stay out of my way!" Kelly hissed on Saturday morning. Putting her hands on her hips, she glared at Maya.

A few feet away, Maya glared back, her eyes like chips of blue ice. "I am not in *your* way," she said in clipped tones. *"You're* in *my* way."

"What's the problem, girls?" Emma asked. She stopped the CD player and walked onto the carpet.

The Silver Stars were practicing the group routine. Emma had come up with slightly different choreography to make up for Candace's absence. So far practice hadn't been going well.

"Maya keeps bumping into me when we do our front walkovers," Kelly said.

"Kelly is always out of rhythm," Maya shot back. "If she would do her walkover on time, we wouldn't collide."

For a moment Emma looked at Kelly; then she looked

at Maya. "I have an idea," she said. "Let's move you a little farther apart. Then you won't bump each other." She pulled Kelly back a few inches, then Maya. Kathryn, Harry, and Monica also had to adjust their spacing to remain in line.

"One more time," Emma called, walking back to the CD player. "Let's take it from where you do your front walkovers, then your two sashay-glides with the ribbons." She started the music.

The Silver Stars got into position again. This time Kelly and Maya managed to do their front walkovers without knocking into each other. But when they started their sashay-glides around the edge of the carpet, their ribbons somehow got tangled up.

"Now look what you've done!" Kelly cried. "Watch what you're doing with your ribbon!"

"It isn't my fault," Maya insisted. "You're too slow!"

The music came to an abrupt stop, and all the Silver Stars halted in their tracks.

When Kelly saw her mother's face, she swallowed hard.

"Uh-oh," Monica whispered next to Kelly.

"You two seem unable to work together," Emma said calmly to Maya and Kelly. Kelly could tell her mother's patience was wearing thin.

"It's her fault—" Kelly began.

"She's too slow," Maya interrupted.

Holding up her hands for silence, Emma waited until she had everyone's attention. "This is a group routine," she reminded them. "You must perform as a unit. If you can't find a way to work together, then perhaps neither of you should participate."

"But we need five people for the team," Kelly said. "Without Candace, there're only five of us left."

"That's correct," Emma said. "So what will happen if I have to sideline the two of you?"

"Our team won't be able to compete," Maya said in a small voice.

"That's right," Emma said. "So it comes down to this; you two keep your differences out of this gym, or the Silver Stars are out of the Strawberry Festival. Got it?"

"Got it," Kelly muttered, an embarrassed flush staining her cheeks.

"Got it," Maya responded softly, gazing at her bare feet.

"Good," Emma said. "Now, I'm going to start this music one last time. You two do your parts, or this group routine is out. I'm not going to waste my time or your teammates' time by practicing something that won't work." Turning her back on them, Emma strode to the portable CD player.

Kelly swallowed and looked at Monica. Monica had a desperate look on her face.

"Please," she whispered to Kelly. "Please don't ruin it for everyone."

Kelly swallowed hard again. The other Silvers were counting on her and Maya. Her feelings toward Maya would have to be kept in the locked box. At least until after the Festival.

The first notes of the music started again, and the Silver

Stars quickly got into position. Kelly concentrated on her movements and refused to think about Maya except as another body she had to move around.

They didn't bump during the walkovers.

Their ribbons didn't get tangled.

The Silver Stars made it all the way through their routine with no mistakes.

As the music faded, Kelly breathed a sigh of relief. Now she just had to keep that box locked. Even if it was bulging at the sides.

———————

"So, I saw Maya messing up during your group practice," Julie said casually as Kelly took a drink of water.

Wiping her mouth, Kelly nodded.

"She sure isn't as great as she says she is," Julie said. She leaned over and drank from the fountain. "The other day she was complaining about how you were so full of yourself that you were ruining the whole team event."

Kelly's lips pressed together. "It isn't me," she said. "It's her. She doesn't know what she's doing."

"Oh, I know," Julie said, shaking her head. "I have eyes. Since she's come here, she's just sort of ruined everything, huh? Once she even said that Emma will start loving her more than she loves you." Julie looked sympathetic.

"No way," Kelly said tightly. "I know my mom loves me more."

"Really? Well, that's great. You just keep telling yourself that," Julie said. Then she pointed across the gym. Over by the balance beam, Emma had her arm around Maya's shoulders. She was saying something, and Maya was nodding. Soon a wide smile spread across Maya's face.

Well, that's a first, Kelly thought. Inside, her heart felt as if it were turning to ice.

————————

"One and two and step-kick and glide," Kelly muttered. It was almost nine o'clock on Tuesday night, and Kelly knew that soon her mother would come downstairs and ask her to get ready for bed. Since Kelly and Maya had been arguing constantly, their parents were still encouraging them to give each other space. Maya was allowed to use the basement exercise room from seven until eight, and Kelly had it from eight to nine. It wasn't long enough for Kelly.

"Hold Me Forever" was playing on the tape player, and Kelly was practicing some of the dance-type movements of her solo routine. Sighing, she wiped her face with a clean towel. She had gone over these movements fifty times so far, but she wanted to get them even smoother and more graceful—absolutely perfect. In the big mirror on one wall, she saw her feet do the little skips and slides automatically. Kelly concentrated on her arms, hands, and wrists. Maybe if she did a little body wave here . . .

————————

"This week has really stunk so far," Kelly complained on Wednesday afternoon. She pulled her textbooks out of her locker and slammed the door. "And it's only half over."

Monica wrinkled her nose. "Ms. Reynolds, is that 'stunk' in the past perfect, or is it 'stank'? Or did you mean, 'This week has really been stinking,' which would be the continuing present imperfect?"

Kelly giggled and swatted at Monica's shoulder with one hand. "You are so weird," she said.

"That's why you like me," Monica said smugly.

"Yeah," Kelly admitted. She and Monica began trudging down the hall to the library, where they both had study hall.

"How are things at home?" Monica asked as they shuffled along with the stream of students.

"Tense," Kelly said. "Last night she banged on my wall for me to turn my music down. And I wasn't even playing Skyrocket all that loud. But she said she couldn't study, and I said she should go downstairs . . ."

Monica whistled. "Sounds bad."

"It was. Then this morning she was hogging the bathroom for hours, so *I* banged on *that* door until she got out."

"Whew," Monica breathed. "Your folks must be going crazy."

"They're trying to stay out of it. But I keep seeing them giving each other worried glances." Kelly pushed open the library door, and she and Monica found an empty table. Busily, they spread out their books, opened their notebooks and assignment pads, and looked very studious. Then they dropped their heads behind their textbooks and whispered.

"You guys did okay at SGA yesterday, though," Monica

87

said softly. "I was really worried about the group routine for a while. But now I think it's going to be great—if you and Maya can keep it together. How do you feel about your solo?"

Kelly smiled. "I'm happy with it. Mom has been working with me on the back somi, and I'm nailing it practically every time. So I know I can do it in competition. And tonight, Maya and Mom are going to go home by themselves so that Dimitri and I can stay late to work on it on the regulation beam."

"Good," Monica whispered. "Dimitri's really nice, huh?"

"Yeah." Kelly looked wistful. "Too bad his daughter isn't. Hey, have you talked to Candace lately? Yesterday I asked her why she wasn't eating lunch with us anymore, and she acted like I wasn't even there."

Monica shook her head. "She did the same thing to me. I talked to Kathryn about it, and she said Candace is just embarrassed. I wish she'd come back to class. I mean, she made me crazy, but she was fun. She helped lighten things up."

"Yeah. Problem is sometimes she took things a little *too* lightly. I know what you mean, though. I miss her too."

Chapter Seventeen

That evening, Kelly looked in the fruit basket on the kitchen counter. She was starving, even though they'd had dinner only two hours before. "Wasn't there one last peach?" she murmured to herself.

Pushing through the swinging door, she headed down the hallway to the living room. Before Emma and Dimitri had gotten married, Kelly and Emma had lived in a two-bedroom condo in downtown Atlanta. Now the four of them lived in a big Victorian house. Kelly was still getting used to having a separate dining room, and a library too.

She found Maya stretched out on the floor in the foyer, reading the newspaper. She was eating a peach.

"You took the last peach!" Kelly said accusingly.

Maya looked up. "So what?" she asked, her eyes narrowing.

"So you're selfish, that's what! You could have asked first." Kelly felt her anger start to build inside her.

"I don't have to ask you if I can eat something. Your

name wasn't written on this peach," Maya said, her chin sticking out. "That's how you are—you think everything belongs to you. You're the selfish one!"

"*What?*" Kelly shrieked.

"Girls!" Dimitri said, his deep voice sounding like thunder.

Kelly jumped and turned to face her stepfather. Maya sat up quickly.

Dimitri's normally smiling face looked unhappy. "Please keep apart until you can talk peacefully with each other."

Emma came down the stairs and put an arm around Dimitri's waist. He squeezed her hand, still looking upset.

"Kelly, if you're still hungry, there are some frozen fruit bars in the freezer," she said. "Or you can make popcorn."

"Fine," Kelly snapped. "I'll make popcorn." Turning sharply, she stomped back to the kitchen.

She rattled the pot as loudly as she could. With any luck, Maya loved popcorn and would be dying for some. And Kelly would say no.

————

"Okay, people!" Emma called on Thursday afternoon. She clapped her hands. "Let's go through it one more time!"

The five Silver Stars assumed their positions.

Emma went to the rolling stand that held the sound equipment, and flipped a switch. The first few notes of "Colors of the Wind" filtered through the speakers.

Harry and Maya ran onto the carpet, followed by Kelly, Kathryn, and Monica. They met in the middle, then split

up, each facing a different direction. The five of them performed back walkovers, then balanced on their forearms
with their feet curled up over their backs. Then they un-
furled their long ribbons, each a different color, and ran
around the edge in a circle.

Even though working with Maya was difficult, Kelly
loved the routine that her mother had choreographed. She
had loved the movie *Pocahontas,* and "Colors of the Wind"
was the most beautiful song she'd ever heard. *Next to
"Hold Me Forever," by Skyrocket,* she thought. Ahead of
her, Maya ran gracefully, her blue ribbon trailing behind
her.

Kelly hated to admit it, but Maya really *was* good.

While all the Silver Stars had talent, Kelly knew without
being conceited that she had always stood out. She had
natural ability, and she was dedicated. The other Silvers
weren't quite as obsessive about details and perfection.

But Maya was. Her every movement was crisp and exact. She did each move perfectly, again and again. For the
first time, someone Kelly's age was just as good as Kelly.
And she hated, hated, hated it.

Holding her own yellow ribbon high, Kelly ran around
the carpet, trying to keep exactly halfway between Maya
and Kathryn. Suddenly her eye caught a flash of bright red
hair at the edge of the carpet. Kelly wanted to look, but it
was time to go into the next section of the choreography.

The Silver Stars went through their routine, using their
ribbons to express the emotion of the song. When the music finally stopped, Maya, Kelly, Kathryn, and Monica were

all in tightly curled balls on the carpet, each facing a different direction, their ribbons coiled around them. Harry was in the center, holding a very steady headstand.

The music faded away, and the Silver Stars stood up.

"That was excellent, everyone," Emma said, giving each of them a smile. "Really terrific. You've all worked hard and it shows."

Kelly slapped Monica a high five, and Kathryn hit one with Harry. Harry went to give one to Maya, but Maya just looked at her.

"Come on," Harry coached her. "Hold your hand up like this." She pulled Maya's hand up in the air, then slapped it. "That's called slapping high five," Harry said. "We do it when we're happy. See?"

"Yes." Maya grinned, seeming pleased to know this new custom. "Thank you."

Then Kelly spotted Candace walking toward them. She was congratulating everyone. For the past week Candace had ignored them all and refused all offers to make up. *So why is she here now?* Kelly wondered.

"Hi, Candace," Monica said. "Good to see you again."

"Hi, Monica," Candace said. "Hey, everyone. Hi, Emma." Candace looked down at her feet for a moment.

"Hello, Candace," Emma said with a smile. "Are you here to give the Silver Stars another chance?"

"I was hoping you'd give *me* another chance," Candace said, showing none of her usual brashness. "Since last week I've realized how much I missed coming here, how much it means to me to do gymnastics. I was hoping . . . well, I was hoping I could try again."

"That would be great," Emma said warmly, putting an arm around Candace's shoulder. "We would love to have you back."

Candace's face lit up. "Oh, thanks, Emma! I can run and change right now. I've been practicing the group routine at home, and I'm ready to jump back in."

"Just a moment, Candace," Emma said, her face looking serious. "I'm sorry, but I'm afraid you can't be in the group routine. The others have been practicing the new choreography for a week, and it wouldn't be fair to them to have to change now."

Candace frowned. "But the Strawberry Festival is this weekend. Do you mean I can't do anything at all?"

Emma tapped a finger against her chin, looking thoughtful. "No," she said slowly. "Maybe there *is* something you can do."

———

"See? This is a hot-fudge sundae," Harry explained patiently. "You can get it with butterscotch sauce, or with strawberry instead. And then you mix it all up together and eat it."

Maya watched as Harry took a spoonful of vanilla ice cream, dipped it in the hot fudge at the bottom of her dish, and ate it.

"I see." Maya nodded. She dipped her spoon into her

ice cream and then into her hot fudge. Then she put the spoon in her mouth. Her eyes opened wide. "Oh, this is good," she said. "This is very good."

Harry, Kathryn, and Candace laughed. Kelly and Monica looked away. The six Silver Stars were having a reunion celebration at Gianelli's Ice Cream Shop, and they were all squeezed into the very back booth. Harry was giving Maya more lessons in American culture and customs.

"And see, if you have a straw, you rip off just one end of the wrapper. Like this." Harry demonstrated. "Then you put the straw into your mouth and blow hard. And the paper goes flying! Watch." Harry sent her straw wrapper halfway across Gianelli's. "But you have to do it when no one's looking," she counseled.

"I understand," Maya said. "Thank you for showing me."

For a split second, Kelly felt a twinge of guilt. Maya was *her* stepsister. She should be the one showing Maya all these things to help her fit in. Then she shook her head. She had tried. Maya wasn't interested in being her friend. And once they got through the group routine at the Strawberry Festival, Kelly was going to unlock her box and really let Maya have it. She frowned. The Silver Stars might not be big enough for both of them.

"So our team event looks fabulous," Kathryn said. "It's too bad you can't be in it, Candace."

"Yeah." Candace looked regretful.

"Did Emma come up with something for you to do?" Monica asked. "I thought I heard her tell you something."

To Kelly's surprise, Candace blushed and took a sip of her milk shake. "Um, yeah," she muttered. "I'll be at the Festival."

"Doing what?" Kelly asked.

"It's, well, it's a secret," Candace said.

Monica sat up straighter. "A secret?" she asked, her voice rising.

"Yeah. You'll just have to wait and see," Candace said.

Chapter Eighteen

"Where are we? Where are we?" Harry asked, bouncing a little on her toes.

Kelly pointed to the schedule tacked to a large bulletin board at the entrance of the Strawberry Festival fairgrounds. "Right here. Near the shortcake tent. See? There are times listed for everyone's performances."

Saturday had dawned warm, clear, and sunny—perfect weather for the Festival. When Kelly had woken up, her stomach had already been quivery with excitement and anticipation. This was what she had been working toward for the past two and a half weeks. Would she do well? Was her dismount ready? Would Maya score higher?

At breakfast she had been almost too nervous to eat, but she knew Dimitri and Emma wouldn't let her compete if she didn't. So she'd gagged down a bowl of cereal with fruit. Across the table, Maya had done the same thing. She had circles under her eyes and looked tense.

Always copying me, Kelly thought angrily. *I was nervous first.*

And suddenly here they were, at the fairgrounds for the annual Strawberry Festival. Huge striped tents covered the grassy area, and there were crafts booths and games and even some carnival rides. Everywhere the delicious aroma of sweet, ripe strawberries wafted through the air, tickling Kelly's nose and making her mouth water.

This morning Kelly had come to the fairgrounds early with her mother, which she was glad about. The last thing she'd needed was to ride in the same car as her stepsister. Maya and Dimitri were meeting them here in a few minutes. When Emma and Kelly had arrived, Emma had gone ahead to do a safety check on all the gymnastics equipment that her students would be using.

Now Monica nudged Kelly in an attempt to see the schedule. "Okay, there are going to be simultaneous exhibitions," she read. "I'm on at ten o'clock, at gymnastic area one, and Kelly, you're on at ten-ten. Harry is on at ten also, over by gymnastic area three. Then Kathryn is on at ten-twenty at gymnastic area two."

"What about our group routine?" Kathryn asked.

"Here we are: the Silver Stars of Sugarloaf Gymnastic Academy," Harry said. "We perform at two o'clock, at gymnastic area one." She pointed to the schedule listing their program. "Of course, I brought my lucky hat." She held up a red, white, and blue baseball cap, signed by Mary Lou Retton.

97

"You always say that," Monica teased her. "I think you sleep with that hat."

"Maybe I do," Harry said with a grin. "So what?"

"Ugh, we're on right after the Gold Stars," Kelly interrupted. "With four different schools competing, you'd think we wouldn't have to be right next to *them*."

"Yeah," Monica agreed, hoisting her tote bag onto her shoulder. "Well, come on. Let's get over to the gymnastic area and get warmed up."

"Hi, everyone," Maya called, rushing up to them. She waved good-bye to Julie Stiller, who split off from the group and went to find Emma.

Maya's blond hair was braided tightly against her head, and she was wearing the same leotard as Kelly, Monica, and Harry: navy blue with a silver star on the chest. Over it she had pulled on warm-up pants and a white jean jacket.

"Hi, Maya," Kathryn said. "We were just going over our schedule." She turned back to the bulletin board.

"Here you are," Harry said, pointing. "Your solo routine is at eleven o'clock at gymnastic area two. Our group exhibition is at two o'clock."

"Okay, okay," Maya murmured, looking at the board. "I'm very nervous—I hardly slept at all last night."

"That's funny," Kelly sniped. "It must have been some stranger snoring in your room, then. You kept *me* up half the night."

Maya's eyes blazed. "I did not!" she cried. "I don't snore. And anyway, I was too nervous to sleep. I told you."

It was stupid to argue, Kelly knew. Getting upset before

they performed was the worst thing they could do. But she couldn't help herself. All the emotions of the past two weeks—no, the past *month*, ever since Maya and Dimitri had come to live with her—came boiling to the surface. She thought about all the things Maya had told Julie, and all the times she had acted so superior and unfriendly.

"Not only did you snore, but then I heard weird thumping noises. What were you doing, shadowboxing?" Kelly put her hands on her hips and glared at Maya.

"Uh, Kelly . . . ," Monica mumbled, tugging on Kelly's warm-up jacket. "We have to compete soon."

Kelly ignored her.

"It's none of your business!" Maya snapped. "You don't own me like you own everything else. But if you really want to know, I was practicing my routine. So that I can beat you here today!"

"Beat me!" Kelly shrieked. "No way! You're crazy!"

"You guys," Kathryn said urgently. "Come on! You're going to ruin it for all of us! Please!"

"I know you've been telling everyone how much better you are than me, but you're not!" Maya cried. "I know you've been telling everyone that Russians aren't as good as Americans. Today I'll show you how wrong you are!"

"What?" Kelly frowned, distracted from her anger for a moment. "I never said that about Russians. But what about you? You've been telling everyone I'm totally stuck up and full of myself!"

"I have not!" Maya said. "You just want to blame me. But Julie told me all the things you've been saying."

"What?" Kelly repeated angrily. "The things *I've* been saying? I haven't been saying anything."

"Sure." Maya sneered. "Pretend you don't know what I'm talking about."

"I don't," Kelly insisted. "But Julie told *me* all about how you think you're so much better, and that you even said my mother is going to love you more than me!"

Shock turned Maya's eyes dark. "What?" she said in a much lower tone. "I never said that. Never, ever."

"Uh-oh," Kathryn said softly. The other Silver Stars were staring at Maya and Kelly in dismay.

Something in Maya's expression told Kelly she was telling the truth. Confusion swirled through her head. "Julie said that you said we were all lame, and that now that you're here, you'll show us what gymnastics really is," Kelly said slowly, relating what Julie had whispered to her a few days ago.

Maya's face looked stricken. "I didn't say that, Kelly. But Julie told me that *you* said that I thought I was so much better than everyone else. She said that you said that Russians were stupid, and that they could never beat Americans."

"Whoa," Monica breathed.

Kelly shook her head. "I never said that, Maya," she said solemnly. "I swear."

"This is too weird," Harry said. "Just what is going on here?"

Chapter Nineteen

"It was Julie," Kelly said. "It was Julie all along."

"But she was so nice," Maya said, her expression confused. "She would say nice things to me, and then she would tell me the awful things you said. Just this morning—"

"She did the same thing to me," Kelly said with a nod. "And she would even"—Kelly was embarrassed to admit it—"get me to say mean things about you. Things I don't think I would have said on my own."

"Me too." Maya looked ashamed.

"But why?" Monica asked. "Why would she go to so much trouble?"

"I know why," Kathryn said suddenly.

Four Silver Stars turned to look at her.

"Think about it," Kathryn said. "Kelly's always been the best Silver Star. I mean, we're all good in different ways, but Kelly's been doing it longer and working harder at it. But now there's Maya too. And she's as good as Kelly."

Kelly and Maya looked at each other. Kelly still felt embarrassed about the whole situation.

"I still don't understand why Julie would do it, though," she said.

"Because of the Gold Stars," Kathryn said, as if it was obvious. "Because we have *both* Kelly and Maya, the Silver Stars are better than ever. Good enough to beat the Gold Stars at the team competition. Unless the Silver Stars are arguing so much that they can't work together. See?"

"Ohhh . . ." The light of understanding started to filter into Kelly's brain.

"Excuse me," Monica said. "I just want to say that I think *all* of us have gotten a ton better in the past year. I mean, maybe we're *all* kind of a threat to the Gold Stars." She played with the zipper on her warm-up jacket, looking self-conscious.

"That's true," Kelly said immediately. "We're all doing great this year—until lately. And Julie picked on me and Maya because we're strangers. It wouldn't have worked with anyone else because we all know each other too well. Julie was playing off our family situation."

Maya nodded. "And it worked. I've been so unhappy, I haven't been doing my best work."

"Me too," Kelly said.

"But now that we know about it, what can we do?" Harry asked.

"You know what they say," Kelly said, her eyes narrowing. "Winning is the best revenge."

"Yeah!" Monica cried, slapping Kelly a high five.

"Me, me!" Maya said, holding up her hand to slap. "I can do five too."

Kelly slapped Maya a humongous high five. "Silver Stars, unite!" she yelled.

———

"I can't believe they put us next to the shortcake tent," Kathryn grumbled.

"I know what you mean," Monica moaned, looking longingly at the rows of strawberry shortcakes awaiting judging. "I can smell them from here, and it's making me crazy. All that whipped cream—ummm."

"After we compete, we can come back and stuff our faces," Kelly said consolingly. "I feel like I need a treat to help me recover from that stunt that Julie pulled. I just hope Maya and I can forget about it during the group event."

"I'm sure y'all will be fine," Monica said. "Now that you know what's going on."

"You don't have to let Julie pull your strings anymore," said Kathryn understandingly.

"Thanks." Kelly nodded. "Oh, Kathryn, I've been meaning to ask—where's Candace?"

Kathryn's eyes twinkled. "Your mom didn't mention anything?"

"No."

"Well, I get the feeling you're about to find out," Kathryn said, giggling.

"Would you like a flyer, ma'am?" a muffled voice asked in back of Kelly.

Turning around, Kelly was confronted with a large walking strawberry. Or rather, someone in a huge strawberry costume. Two of the small black seeds were cut out for eyeholes, and two slim legs wearing green stockings stuck out the bottom. Two arms encased in a red leotard emerged from holes on the sides. One hand was holding a stack of photocopied flyers.

Kelly took one and saw that it was advertising Sugarloaf Gymnastic Academy, showing their gym and listing the teachers and their phone numbers. She looked up at the strawberry. Two small black seeds looked back at her.

"Candace?" Kelly whispered. "Is that you?"

The strawberry shook—trying to nod, Kelly figured.

"This is how your mom said I could do something at the festival," Candace said in a muffled tone. "I said okay, just to show her I was serious about working hard from now on."

Kelly tried to smother her laughter, but she couldn't. Next to her, Kathryn was still giggling, and Monica was hiding her mouth behind her hand. Kelly patted the strawberry on the back, where she guessed a strawberry would have shoulders.

"You're doing great, Candace," she said. "If this doesn't convince them, nothing will."

The strawberry shook again.

The best thing about a competition, Kelly thought, *is watching everyone else perform.*

It was ten minutes to ten, and she, Maya, and Monica were by gymnastic area one.

"Who is that?" Monica asked, checking her program.

"Someone from Rivertown Academy," Kelly told her, not taking her eyes from the performer on the uneven bars. "She's fourteen."

"She's good," Maya said in a soft voice.

Kelly glanced over at her stepsister. Maya looked pale, and her hands were twined together nervously. Even though they had made up, they still had a whole competition to get through.

"Resnikov!" a voice called.

"Here!" Maya whirled to see one of the program judges motioning to her.

"Warm-up," the judge called, gesturing to a regulation balance beam set up on one side. Before each gymnast performed, he or she had to run through his or her routine on the equipment. Kelly and Monica had already done that, since they were about to go on.

Nodding, Maya peeled off her jean jacket and walked over to the beam. Kelly could see the faint curve of her shoulder blades through the navy blue Silver Star leotard.

"Maybe I'll go watch her," Kelly said. "I'll be back before you go on."

"That's a good idea," Monica said softly.

The short green grass of the fairgrounds was already tram-pled flat between the pieces of gymnastics equipment and the large, deep foam mats that surrounded them.

Ahead of her, Maya had begun her practice. On the beam, she pivoted, as Kelly had seen her do many times before. But Maya wavered a little bit. Kelly blinked and stopped about ten feet away. In class her stepsister was always totally in control—she hardly ever fell off or even wobbled. But here she was wobbling only an hour before she was to compete.

Maya caught herself and went down into a backward somersault on the beam, grabbing both sides of it and pull-ing herself over in a smooth movement. Then she went into a straddle split, and then into a handstand.

Kelly tried to send her good vibes. But then it hap-pened.

Maya started to come out of her handstand, but again she wobbled on the way down. She tried to correct her grip, but it was too late. With a dismayed expression on her face, she lost her balance and fell sideways onto the mats beneath her.

Kelly was running to Maya before she even thought about it. When she reached her stepsister, she stood over her, holding out a hand. Maya's face looked white and shaken, and Kelly knew it was from worry and tension. The mats were too thick for the fall to have hurt her.

"Here," Kelly said. "Let me give you a hand."

For a moment Maya looked at her; then her mouth

turned up in a tiny smile. She put her hand out, and Kelly pulled her to her feet.

"I don't know why I fell," Maya said shakily.

"I do," Kelly said. "It's because everything's new, and you feel strange. But you shouldn't feel strange. You're a great gymnast, in Russia or in Atlanta. You belong here as much as anyone."

Maya's eyes lit up. "Do you really think so?" she asked in a soft voice.

Kelly nodded. "I have something to say to you," she began hesitantly. "I'm sorry about the last two weeks. I was stupid to let Julie do that to me. To us." Kelly exhaled deeply and only then realized that she had been holding her breath. It suddenly felt as if a huge weight had been lifted off her shoulders.

"I'm sorry too," Maya said. "I've been so unhappy here—not because of you, at least not at first—but because I'm so homesick. I miss my friends and my grandmother and my school and my gym. When I came here, and you tried to talk to me, I was too unhappy to open up."

"Oh, Maya," Kelly said. A warm feeling of happiness and relief spread through her. Maybe she and her stepsister could be friends after all.

"And I'm not used to how you do things here," Maya went on. "Everything is new, as you said. I know I haven't been very friendly. But I'm sorry about it now."

"Let's just start over from the beginning," Kelly said. "Hi, Maya! I'm Kelly. I'm really glad you and your dad have come to live with us."

107

Maya grinned. "Hi. I'm Maya. I'm really glad to be here—now."

After hesitating a second, Kelly leaned forward and hugged Maya, and Maya hugged her back. They smiled at each other. Then Kelly got businesslike.

"Now, get up on that beam and do another run-through," she said briskly. "And when it's time for your performance, knock their socks off."

Maya frowned. "Why wouldn't I want the judges to wear socks?"

Chapter Twenty

"All right!" Kelly yelled as Monica left the mat and headed over to the sidelines. Monica had just completed her last vault, the handspring with a full turn, and hadn't even wobbled on her landing.

Kelly was clapping hard along with the rest of the crowd.

Smiling, Monica came over to the sidelines. Emma was there, and when Monica came over, Emma gave her a big hug.

"Terrific, sweetie," Emma said. "You did just great. Great landing."

"Thanks," Monica said, smiling self-consciously. "Now we just have to see if the judges agree with you."

Within a minute, the judges had nodded to each other, and a woman stepped up to a microphone on their table.

"The composite score," she read, "for Monica Hales of Sugarloaf Gymnastic Academy is nine point seven."

"All right!" Kelly shouted, patting Monica on her back.

Monica wiggled her eyebrows, looking pleased.

Then Emma turned to Kelly. "You're up next, honey."

Kelly nodded, taking off her light windbreaker. She walked over to the beam and stood about fifteen feet away. As she waited for the judges to signal, she took several deep, calming breaths, focusing her concentration. Just before she started her routine, she glanced at her mom. Emma smiled at her and gave her a thumbs–up. Maya had joined Emma and Monica, and she gave Kelly a tiny nod and a smile.

Then Kelly began.

She ran lightly to the springboard by the side of the beam, bounced once, and landed on the beam in a perfect straddle split with her hands gripping the beam on each side. Keeping her arms straight and stiff, she rose into a steady handstand, then slowly did a back walkover. From a standing position, she sashayed down the length of the beam, then stopped at the end and held a "stork" position to show her balance. After a pirouette, she did a controlled split jump, landing solidly on both feet. When she was almost at the end of the beam, she did a one-handed cartwheel and landed with just inches to spare. After another pirouette, a forward pike somersault was next, then a forward split, then another handstand. In a standing position, she pivoted again, using a little dancelike hop.

This is it. Here goes.

Kelly took a deep breath. She faced away from the end of the beam and thought about all the times she had practiced the back somi dismount. Then she coiled down and sprang backward, snapping her feet through the air. The

110

mat rushed up to meet her, and she straightened her legs, keeping her knees loose. Suddenly she was landing hard on both feet. She steadied herself, straightened up as tall as she could, and threw her hands over her head.

Touchdown.

The crowd surrounding the beam started yelling and clapping.

I did it, Kelly thought proudly.

While everyone clapped and yelled her name, Kelly trotted off the mats toward her mother, Monica, and Maya.

Stepping forward, Emma folded Kelly into a hug and kissed the top of her head. "Honey, that was fantastic," she told her. "I've never seen you do better. And your dismount looked terrific."

Kelly smiled, feeling a little embarrassed, the way she always did when someone complimented her. "Thanks, Mom," she said.

Then Monica came and slapped her a high five. "Go, girl," Monica said, shaking her hand as if Kelly were too hot to touch.

There was one more person to talk to. Kelly looked around and saw Maya standing off to one side. Maya was smiling but looked unsure.

"That was wonderful, Kelly," Maya said.

"Did I look like a falcon?" Kelly asked with a grin.

Maya nodded. "Yeah. Exactly."

"Good luck with your routine," Kelly said.

"Thanks," Maya replied.

Then the judges signaled that they were ready with

Kelly's score. The same female judge who had announced Monica's score stepped up to the microphone again.

"The composite score for Kelly Reynolds of Sugarloaf Gymnastic Academy is nine point six," she said.

Kelly nodded happily, feeling as if her face would split if her smile got any bigger. A score of nine point six was very good. This Strawberry Festival was turning out great.

"Come on—I want to be at the front of the crowd," Kelly said, tugging on Harry's arm.

With Monica and Kathryn on Kelly's other side, the four of them hurried to gymnastic area one, where Maya would perform. For the past forty minutes, they had been wandering around the Festival. Since they had all already done their solo routines, they could sample some of the strawberry-themed food. Kelly and Kathryn had gone for the shortcake, while Harry had tried the strawberry pie and Monica had wolfed down a sugar cookie topped with strawberry jam.

"What time is it?" Monica asked, still licking her fingers.

"Two minutes to eleven," Kelly said, pushing through the crowd.

At gymnastic area one, Dimitri was standing ready to spot Maya on the beam. The judges were seated behind a folding table about twenty feet away, where they would have a good view.

Kelly found Susan Lu in the crowd and went to stand

next to her. Emma was over at gymnastic area three, where some of the Gold Stars were competing.

Maya was already at her starting point, waiting for the judges' signal. Kelly could see she was breathing deeply and slowly, and her eyes were locked on the beam. *She's going through her routine in her head,* Kelly realized. Kelly did the same thing before a performance.

Looking up for a split second, Maya caught Kelly's eye, and Kelly quickly gave her a thumbs–up. Maya looked so tense that she didn't even respond. Kelly bit her lip, remembering how nervous Maya had been and how she had fallen off the beam earlier.

Then the judges signaled Maya, and Maya ran toward the springboard. After one bounce she landed on the beam in a squat, only barely using her hands to steady herself. From there she flowed into a forward somersault, then into a handstand, which she used to pirouette. This was where she had fallen off before, and Kelly held her breath until Maya sank into a backward somersault.

That's a really hard move, Kelly thought. *I'm going to try that on Tuesday.*

The rest of Maya's routine went smoothly. She did a cartwheel and a series of sashays. For her jump she did a quick tuck jump, but wobbled a teensy bit on her landing. Kelly hoped the judges hadn't noticed. Then Maya did a series of step kicks to the other end of the beam to get ready for her dismount.

Maya stood at the very end of the beam, facing the

opposite direction. Kelly saw Maya's fists clench as she focused on what she was about to do. Then, just as Kelly had done, she coiled down, pumped her arms, and snapped her body backward, all at the same time. Flying into the air, she left the beam behind, then uncurled and got her legs under her in the right position to land. With her knees bent to absorb the impact, Maya landed on the thick mats behind the beam.

Kelly saw that she planted her feet right away and didn't wobble even a little bit. Then Maya straightened up, arched her back, and raised her arms over her head.

"Good!" Kelly exclaimed, grabbing Monica's arm. "She did great!"

"Yeah, that was really nice." Monica nodded. "But she wobbled on her tuck jump."

Dimitri clapped for his daughter and put an arm around her as she picked up her jean jacket and came over to join the others.

"Terrific, Maya," Susan said, smoothing Maya's hair.

"Thank you," Maya said shyly. "I messed up my tuck jump."

"I bet no one noticed," Kelly said loyally. "Everything else you did was perfect. Especially your back somi dismount."

Maya smiled at her, and Kelly felt as if the strain of the last several weeks had melted away.

Soon the judge stood up to give them Maya's score. "The composite score for Maya Resnikov," she announced, "is nine point four."

Kelly couldn't believe her ears. They had definitely noticed Maya's wobble on her tuck jump. She'd thought that Maya would get a nine point seven at least. Anxiously she looked over to see how Maya was taking it.

"It's a fair score," Maya said with a shrug. "I did my best, but I was really nervous. You know, it was my first American meet."

"You still looked like a falcon, Maya," Kelly said.

Maya grinned. "Yeah. I made them take off their socks, right?"

"What?" Monica asked, looking confused.

Kelly laughed. "I know what Maya means." She took Maya's arm. "Come on. I want to introduce you to an important American custom: eating strawberry shortcake."

Chapter Twenty-one

"Wow. That's really something, huh?" Harry asked on Tuesday afternoon.

"Sure is," Kelly agreed. They were standing in front of the big glass case at SGA, where all the trophies were kept. Right in the middle of the second shelf was a tall gold statue of a girl leaping into the air. The girl was attached to a wooden frame, and at the bottom of the frame was a small brass plaque. It said:

SECOND PLACE—GROUP EXHIBITION

ATLANTA STRAWBERRY FESTIVAL

THE SILVER STARS OF SUGARLOAF GYMNASTIC ACADEMY

Sighing, Harry pressed her face against the glass. "I wish it said first place instead of second."

"Too bad Rivertown did so well," Kelly said. "We'll beat 'em next time. At least it doesn't say third place. Right,

Julie?" The Gold Stars had placed third and a team from Dynamic Gymnasts fourth.

"Oh, shut up," Julie Stiller said, passing them with her head held high. Kelly and Harry laughed.

The double glass doors opened behind Kelly, and Maya, Monica, and Kathryn rushed in.

"Are we late?" Monica cried, tugging off her sneaker as she hopped on one foot. "We were all stuck on the same slow bus."

"Relax," Kelly said, laughing. "I think you have a whole minute to change. You don't have to do a striptease in front of the whole gym."

The five Silver Stars headed back to the girls' locker room.

"The Strawberry Festival was fun," Kathryn said, her ponytail bobbing behind her.

"I liked our group routine, even though we didn't win," Monica said. "I love learning new moves."

"Yeah," Kelly said with a nod. She glanced at Maya and gave her a smile. "But the group routine wasn't the only thing I learned for that meet."

Maya grinned and gave a little skip. Then she looked around the gym, and her face became sober.

"Uh-oh," she said. "I think maybe *we* learned something, but someone else didn't. Where's Candace? Is she starting her new chance by being late to class?"

Kelly looked around, but didn't see the sixth Silver Star. "Oh no," she groaned. "Mom's really going to let her have it now!"

Kathryn shook her head. "This is so typical," she groused. "It's always the same thing with her. I've never known anyone so laz—"

"Hey, guys," Candace said calmly, coming out of the girls' locker room. She was in a blue leotard, and her curly red hair was pulled neatly back with a hair elastic. "Where have you been? You're almost late. Hurry up and get changed. I'll meet you over by the mirrors."

Kelly's jaw dropped. Monica shook her head. Harry and Kathryn stared at each other, then back at Candace, who was swooping down in big movements, limbering up for class.

"Well," Maya said, speaking up first. "I guess we *all* did learn something at the Strawberry Festival."

Laughing, the five Silver Stars turned and trooped into the locker room to change.

ABOUT THE AUTHOR

Gabrielle Charbonnet was born and raised in New Orleans, where she now lives with her husband, daughter, and two spoiled cats, Rufus and Fidel. She has written several other middle-grade books, as well as numerous books under a pseudonym.

When she was younger, she loved gymnastics as much as the Silver Stars do.

Gymnastic Moves and Positions

Aerial: any gymnastic skill that is performed without the hands touching the floor, such as an aerial cartwheel or aerial walkover.

Back handspring: a back flip of the body onto both hands, with both legs following as a pair. The gymnast begins and ends in a standing position.

Back somersault: a backward roll on the floor or beam, with knees in the tucked position. (The aerial version of this move is called a back salto.)

Back somi dismount: a dismount from the beam using an aerial back somersault.

Back walkover: a move made from a back-arch (or bridge) position, bringing one foot, then the other, down toward the front. Similar to a back handspring but using smoother, more controlled movements and moving arms and legs one at a time rather than in pairs.

Cartwheel: an easy move, in which the hands are placed on the ground sideways, one after the other, with each leg following. Arms and legs should be straight.

Front handspring: a forward flip onto both hands, with both legs following as a pair. The gymnast begins and ends in a standing position.

Front hip pullover: a mount used on the uneven

parallel bars. The body is supported on the hands, the hips resting on either bar. Usually combined with a hip circle.

Front pike somersault: a forward somersault in which the knees are kept straight.

Front somersault: a forward body roll on the floor or beam, with knees in the tucked position. (The aerial form of this move is called a salto.)

Front split: a split in which one leg is forward, one back.

Front walkover: a move made from a front-split handstand position, bringing one foot, then the other, down toward the back. Similar to a front handspring but using smoother, more controlled movements and moving arms and legs one at a time rather than in pairs.

Handstand: a move performed by supporting the body on both hands, with the arms straight and the body vertical.

Hip circle: a move made by circling either bar of the uneven parallel bars with the hips touching the bar. If the hips do not touch the bar, the move is called a clear hip circle.

Kip: a move performed on the uneven parallel bars; the gymnast moves from a hanging position to a position supported by the hands.

Layout: extending the body to its full length, usually during an aerial move.

Sticking: refers to a dismount or final move that is performed without taking additional steps.

Pike: any move in which the body is bent and the knees are kept straight.

Roundoff: similar to a cartwheel, but with a half-twist and the legs together. The gymnast ends facing the direction she started from.

Skin-the-cat: a swing movement on the uneven parallel bars, in which both of the gymnast's legs pass through her arms as she hangs from either bar.

Stork position: a standing position in which the gymnast balances on one leg.

Straddle: a position in which the gymnast's legs are far apart at each side.

Straddle split: a split with legs out at each side. This move is used in all four women's events.

Straddle swing: a swing movement on the uneven parallel bars in which the legs are extended at each side.

Tuck: a move in which the knees are brought to the chest.

Bantam Books invites you to read
a dynamic new series,

AMERICAN GOLD SWIMMERS

by Sharon Dennis Wyeth

AMERICAN GOLD SWIMMERS

A Series by Sharon Dennis Wyeth

#1 *The Winning Stroke*
CHAPTER 6

"That's two seconds off my original time," said Kristy as she climbed out of the pool the next day. "Must be my lucky goggles."

"The freestyle is a good stroke for you," said Coach Apple.

"It's my favorite," said Kristy. "I wish I were swimming in the hundred free tonight at the meet."

"I need you to swim the backstroke," said the coach. "You're good there too. Donna and Mary June will swim the hundred free in the eleven- and twelve-year-old girls' group."

"Whatever you say, Coach," said Kristy.

The coach handed Kristy a towel. "Whatever you do, don't forget to wear those goggles at our meet tonight!"

Kristy felt a tap on her shoulder. Rosa stood

there, pale and dripping. "I was a little faster in the breaststroke," she said, panting. "Donna timed me."

"Great," said Kristy.

"I guess so," said Rosa. "But I'm really nervous about tonight."

"I'm not nervous at all," said Kristy as they headed for the locker room.

"I guess I've just got a lot going on," explained Rosa. "Tonight's meet. And tomorrow afternoon's dance program."

"Can I come and watch you dance?" asked Kristy.

Rosa smiled. "Sure. My mom will tell the box office to put aside a ticket for you."

"Make that two tickets," Kristy said with a mischievous look in her eye. "I'll see if someone else I know can come."

Kristy and Rosa dressed for class. Then Rosa stood under the hair dryer. "How did Kirk do in his meet for the Dolphins last night?" she asked over the noise of the dryer.

"He came in second in the four-hundred-yard back," Kristy replied.

Rosa sighed and combed out a tangle. "Did you tell him anything?" she asked loudly.

"About what?" Kristy asked, tying her sneaker.

"About me!" Rosa yelled over the sound of the dryer.

"Of course not," said Kristy. She got up and stood next to Rosa at the mirror. "But when I got home last night, I did something that I think might help."

"What's that?" asked Rosa as the hair dryer clicked off.

"I'll show you later," said Kristy. "It's in my locker."

Rosa walked away from the mirror and Mary June took her place.

"Your brother was great last night," Mary June said casually as she dabbed on lip gloss.

"Thanks," said Kristy, avoiding her eyes.

"Were you at Kirk's meet?" asked Rosa.

"I'm on the Dolphins myself now," said Mary June. "I told you they'd take me," she boasted. "The Dolphins are a very competitive team and they can really use a swimmer like me in our age group."

Kristy turned away and rolled her suit up in a towel.

"Of course Kristy could probably get on the Dolphins," Mary June said. "Kirk could use his influence."

"Kristy is a good swimmer on her own," Rosa

piped up. "She can make the Dolphins without Kirk."

"I didn't mean to insult anyone," Mary June huffed. She fastened her barrette and spun around. Sweeping past the bench, she knocked Kristy's goggles on the floor.

"Hey, watch out!" cried Kristy.

"It's only a pair of goggles," said Mary June.

Kristy picked up the goggles and brushed them off. "It just so happens that my brother gave them to me," she explained. "And they're lucky."

Mary June smiled smugly. "Well then, you'd better wear them tonight. You'll need all the luck you can get."

Kristy shook her head as she and Rosa hurried into the hall. "I can't believe her," Kristy said. "Thanks for sticking up for me."

"That's okay," said Rosa. "I think she's jealous of you."

"Why would she be?" asked Kristy. "She's the one the coach is putting in the hundred-yard free. The freestyle is my favorite stroke."

"Listen, Mary June knows you're good," said Rosa. "And I don't think she's too sure of herself."

"But she's always bragging," said Kristy.

"That's my point," said Rosa. "My mother says people who really feel confident don't brag. If Mary

June believes she's a good swimmer, why does she have to keep telling us about it? Don't let her get to you."

"I'll try, but she makes it hard," Kristy said as they got to her locker. She spun the lock, opened the door, and took out a rolled-up poster. "Remember I told you that I had an idea to get Kirk to like you?" Holding it up, she said, "Look at this!"

Just at that moment, Kirk and Jonah walked by.

"Come here, Kirk," called Kristy.

The boys strolled over. Rosa leaned against the bank of lockers and smiled at Kirk.

"Look what Rosa made for you," Kristy announced, shoving the rolled-up poster at her brother.

Kirk looked at Rosa. "What is it?"

Rosa stammered, "I'm not . . . not sure—"

"She's not sure you'll like it," Kristy said quickly. She took the poster back from Kirk and unrolled it. "It's a campaign poster for the Student Council election," explained Kristy. "Rosa wasn't sure what you'd think, but I really like it."

Rosa glanced at the poster and then shot Kristy a grateful look. Kirk took the poster and held it up. There was a picture of a diver on a board and a slogan in rainbow colors.

Jonah read the slogan out loud and chuckled. " 'Vote for unsinkable Kirk Adams! It's unthinkable not to!' "

"Hey! That's cool," said Kirk. "Gee, thanks, Rosa."

"You're welcome," Rosa said, looking down at her toes.

The bell rang. Kirk tucked the poster under his arm, and he and Jonah hurried away.

"Don't forget the party at my house tonight," Jonah called back to Kristy and Rosa before he turned the corner.

When Kristy and Rosa got to English class, Ms. Bartlett was handing back homework.

"I loved your story, Kristy," Ms. Bartlett said, placing a paper on Kristy's desk. "The part about the blond girl at the pool who turns into a shark was hysterical." Kristy smiled and tucked the paper in her notebook.

After class, Rosa grabbed Kristy in the hall.

"Thanks for saying that I made the campaign poster for Kirk," said Rosa.

"He seemed to like it," said Kristy.

"I feel guilty for taking the credit, though."

"It is kind of dishonest," Kristy admitted. "I'd planned to say that we did it together. But then when Kirk showed up, I got carried away with my own brilliant scheme. And you have to admit, it was brilliant!"

"You're right," said Rosa. "But maybe we shouldn't tell lies."

"It was only a fib," said Kristy. "Besides, I had my fingers crossed behind my back."

When Kristy got home from school that afternoon, Kirk was already eating.

"Better put something in your stomach now, Kriss," he said. "You can't eat right before you swim tonight, you know."

Kristy stepped over Hamlet and washed her hands at the sink. "I can hardly wait until the meet," she said.

"Aren't you nervous?" asked Kirk.

"Not a bit," said Kristy. "Even though the back isn't my best stroke."

"You'll do fine," said Kirk.

"Thanks," said Kristy. "By the way, Rosa's having a dance program at the college tomorrow afternoon. Want to go?"

"I don't know," said Kirk. "I don't really like dance."

"*Please*," said Kristy. "It would mean a lot to Rosa."

"Okay, I guess," Kirk said with a shrug.

Mr. Adams walked in carrying some costumes. "Wait until you see what I've got for *Hamlet*!" he said.

The yellow Lab raised his head and thumped his tail.

"He's not talking about you," Kristy said to the dog.

Kirk laughed and refilled Hamlet's water bowl. "I'll be glad when your students finish this production, Dad," he said. "You're confusing our dog."

"Sorry, Hamlet," Mr. Adams said, draping the costumes over a chair. "I'm going to go say hi to your mother, kids."

On the way out the door, he hugged Kristy. "I don't think I've told you lately how proud I am that you're on the swim team. Good luck tonight."

Kristy flushed with pleasure and hugged him back. "Thanks, Dad."

That evening Kristy and Kirk left for the pool early. Their parents planned to come after the warm-up.

"Keep your focus," Kirk warned. Then he smiled. "Break a leg tonight, Kriss."

"You too," she said. "See you in the water."

Inside the girls' locker room, Rosa was sitting on the bench already suited up.

"Wow, the team colors look great on you!" Kristy said. Rosa stood up and modeled the suit. It was turquoise with a crimson stripe. The letters sw, for Surfside Waves, were printed in crimson on the front.

"I can't wait to put mine on," Kristy said, tearing into her backpack. She found her team suit and put it on quickly. "It's definitely me," she said, looking in the mirror. "By the way," she told Rosa. "Kirk's coming to your program. He said he loves dance."

"You're kidding," squealed Rosa. "That's fantastic!"

Kristy smiled. "Come on. Let's get a shower."

After showering, the girls went to the pool for a warm-up. Kristy jumped right in. Rosa stuck her toe in the pool and shivered. "It feels cold tonight," she said. "I've got goose bumps. Probably because I'm so nervous."

"There's nothing to be nervous about," Kristy yelled from the water. "All you have to do is jump in."

Coach Apple appeared at the side of the pool. "Don't tire yourself out," she warned Kristy. "Take a deep breath if your stomach does flip-flops."

"My stomach isn't doing flip-flops," said Kristy. "I feel great. I'm not a bit nervous."

After warming up, the girls went back to the

locker room to rest and to eat the granola bars Rosa's mother had packed for them. Kristy took off her goggles and cap and put them on the table next to her locker. Then she and Rosa went to the water fountain. When the girls came back, they saw Mary June and Donna standing near the table chatting.

"Don't you like the team colors?" Donna was saying.

"I like the Dolphin colors better," said Mary June. "The deep blue really brings out the color of my eyes."

Kristy went straight to the table and picked up her cap. She was determined not to let Mary June get to her. "Hey," she said, looking at the empty table, "where are my goggles?"

"Don't worry," said Donna, opening a locker. "I have an extra pair."

"No thanks," said Kristy. "I want *my* goggles. The ones Kirk gave me. They're lucky."

"Where could they be?" Rosa asked, scanning the floor.

Kristy got down on her knees and looked under the table. "I left them with my cap," she said. "They were here two minutes ago."

"Maybe somebody took them by mistake,"

Donna said. She handed Kristy her extra pair. "Take these."

Coach Apple strode into the locker room and clapped her hands to get everyone's attention. "The first event starts in five minutes," she announced. "Take a deep breath. Focus. Pace yourselves. And above all, have a good swim."

The coach came over and gave Kristy a pat. "You're in the second event, Kristy. You'd better go out and get ready."

Kristy gulped and adjusted the strap on Donna's extra goggles.

"Good luck, Kristy," called Rosa. Suddenly Rosa's voice sounded as if it were coming from far away.

"Thanks," Kristy murmured.

She followed several other girls out to the pool. When she saw the packed viewing stands, she was shocked. She wiped the sweat off her forehead and fiddled with Donna's goggles. She scanned the stands looking for her mother and father, but all the faces seemed to blur. Her stomach clenched into a fist as she watched the girls in the first event take their places. A wave of panic washed over her at the blast of the starting beeper. She took a deep breath and sat down with her back against the wall. She hardly saw the race going on right in front of her.

This is ridiculous! she thought. She hadn't been nervous at all before the coach gave her pep talk. Now she felt as if she might throw up any second.

Please don't let that happen, Kristy prayed, looking up. Suddenly she spotted her mother in the stands. Mr. Adams waved and blew a kiss. Kristy smiled back weakly.

Kristy jumped when the loudspeaker crackled. "The next event will be the eleven-to-twelve-year-old women's hundred-yard backstroke," the announcer said.

Kristy stood up. Her heart raced. Her knees felt weak as she walked over to lane six.

"Swimmers, take your positions—"

Kristy slipped into the water and into starting position. At least with the backstroke she wouldn't have to dive. She breathed deeply. She knew she had to stay still until the sound of the beeper.

"Beep!"

Kristy pushed off. She stroked and kicked as hard as she could. Her mind was racing. *Stroke, stroke, stroke* . . . up above was the string of flags. Three and a half more strokes, touch the wall with her hand, then flip turn . . .

Stroke, stroke, stroke . . . Kristy thought about

her goggles. If she didn't find them, Kirk would be mad. She had felt so lucky earlier in the day. Now maybe her luck was gone. Seeing the flags above her, she stroked and touched the wall, then did a neat flip turn.

Stroke, stroke, stroke . . . Kristy thought about Mary June competing tonight in the freestyle. The freestyle was Kristy's best stroke. She pictured Mary June strutting to the starting block. Kristy's mind drifted.

"Ouch!" she screamed, swallowing water. Pain shot through her head. Her hand jerked up to touch it. "Oh, no," she groaned. She'd swum head-first into the wall.

"Are you okay?" Coach Apple was standing above her.

"I have to keep going," said Kristy.

"It's too late," the coach said. "The heat is over." She put out her hand.

Kristy looked down the pool. The other swimmers had already turned and raced to the opposite end. Their times had been clocked. They were getting out of the pool, while Kristy held on to the wall like an idiot. She bit her lip, trying not to cry.

"I'm not hurt," she said as Coach Apple helped her out of the pool.

"I'll get some ice," said the coach. "Can you walk?"

"Sure," said Kristy. She could walk. She just couldn't swim! Her very first meet and she'd messed up.